ANTIQUES CARRY ON

ANTIQUES CARRY ON

Barbara Allan

SEVERN
HOUSE

First world edition published in Great Britain and the USA in 2021
by Severn House, an imprint of Canongate Books Ltd,
14 High Street, Edinburgh EH1 1TE.

Trade paperback edition first published in Great Britain and the USA in 2022
by Severn House, an imprint of Canongate Books Ltd.

severnhouse.com

British Library Cataloguing-in-Publication Data
A CIP catalogue record for this title is available from the British Library.

ISBN-13: 978-0-7278-9081-8 (cased)
ISBN-13: 978-1-78029-784-2 (trade paper)
ISBN-13: 978-1-4483-0522-3 (e-book)

All Severn House titles are printed on acid-free paper.

Typeset by Palimpsest Book Production Ltd.,
Falkirk, Stirlingshire, Scotland.
Printed and bound in Great Britain by
TJ Books Limited, Padstow, Cornwall.

To Michaela Hamilton
who gave Barbara Allan our start

Brandy's quote:
'But surely for everything you love
you have to pay some price'

– Agatha Christie

Mother's quote:
'To have what we would have,
we speak not what we mean'
– Shakespeare, *Measure for Measure*

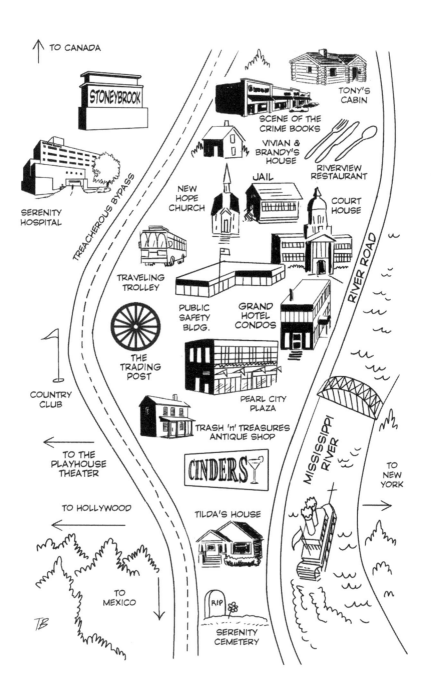

TO CANADA

STONEYBROOK

SERENITY HOSPITAL

TREACHEROUS BYPASS

TRAVELING TROLLEY

THE TRADING POST

COUNTRY CLUB

TO THE PLAYHOUSE THEATER

TO HOLLYWOOD

TO MEXICO

NEW HOPE CHURCH

PUBLIC SAFETY BLDG.

SCENE OF THE CRIME BOOKS

VIVIAN & BRANDY'S HOUSE

JAIL

COURT HOUSE

GRAND HOTEL CONDOS

PEARL CITY PLAZA

TRASH 'n' TREASURES ANTIQUE SHOP

CINDERS

TILDA'S HOUSE

TONY'S CABIN

RIVERVIEW RESTAURANT

RIVER ROAD

MISSISSIPPI RIVER

TO NEW YORK

RIP

SERENITY CEMETERY

TB

ONE
Carry On Girls

Dearest ones!

This is Vivian Borne (a.k.a. Mother) speaking (that is, writing), and where to begin? The beginning, you might well suggest, and we will in fact soon resume at the start of this latest casebook in inspired amateur crime solving.

Of course, some of you already know us well, the two authors of this book that is, while others of you are (as we say in the trade) newbies. So we will commence with yours truly – antiques dealer, legendary local thespian, celebrated amateur sleuth, hearty female of Swedish stock and a certain age (exactly how certain is irrelevant), long widowed, recently retired sheriff, with just a teensy-weensy, hardly-worth-mentioning, hint of bi-polar disorder.

As part of my retirement package as county sheriff, I was given the like-new Vespa, which – despite my having lost my driver's license – was a legal mode of transportation. Correction: I didn't *lose* the card – I knew right where it was! It was just stamped 'revoked' for my having committed various trivial infractions, as when that mailbox practically leapt out in front of me.

The severance package also included a huge send-off party in the ballroom atop the new Merrill Hotel, plus a special honorary sheriff's badge that gets me in most doors. (My daughter Brandy tends to trivialize those honors, but who are you going to believe? An ex-sheriff or her defacto unpaid former deputy?)

I am penning these introductory words from Serenity, Iowa, our small picturesque Midwestern town nestled on the banks of the Mighty Mississippi River. The 'our' of the previous sentence refers to myself and other members of the household

– Brandy (early thirties, divorced, on Prozac, co-author of these books) and her precious little doggie, Sushi (shih tzu, diabetic, and sometime bloodhound).

Now I must impart some important news, and do not mean to alarm our longtime readers, but the time has come for a change.

It is with sadness in our hearts – except for Sushi who understands more than most canines, but certainly not this – that after fifteen years, we bid a fond farewell to our New York publisher, and jump across the pond to a new one in London. (Although, Severn *is* located in the borough of Kensington – a good omen!)

All I will say about the move is that our long-suffering editor must have finally given in to her frustration with my co-narrator's behavior – specifically Brandy's reluctance to get involved in the murder investigations necessary for the continuation of these chronicles, and into which I must drag her screaming and kicking – because the fault certainly couldn't lay (lie?) with *moi*.

Why, everyone knows that I relish a good murder mystery, and seem to attract them like a kitchen magnet to an icebox (an old term, I know, but isn't it evocative?). In fact, our sleepy little burg has set a Guinness World Record for the most murders per capita in the entire United States! Perhaps not the highest honor . . . but still, a rare distinction.

Anywho, this beautiful spring morning I have gone off by myself, while Brandy and Sushi are tending to our antiques shop. The dear girl runs the cash register while security guard Sushi follows customers around making sure no one has sticky fingers, as we deplore any 'check your bags or large purses' or 'smile, you're on camera,' policies. So undignified!

See you next chapter!

Brandy, the 'dear girl,' speaking. For those of you who might have found the preceding paragraphs a bit like chugging condensed milk from the can, I assure you that from here on out I will be handling the lion's share of the narration (as opposed to the lyin' share).

I'm afraid Mother insisted on beginning our story this time, and for you newbies (as she says) I thought perhaps, before the express train leaves the station, fairness required giving you an idea of just what kind of trip you're embarking upon . . . because once this journey starts, there's no way off unless you jump.

Firstly, I think we all know who taxed our former editor to the breaking point, and it wasn't me. Secondly, Mother's short reign of three months as county sheriff ended in a backroom deal in which she agreed to step down in exchange for 1) a *small* retirement party, 2) a *used* Vespa, and 3) an honorary badge one step up from a toy prize in a cereal box.

It was either accept those terms or face impeachment.

Granted, Mother did solve one of the most baffling and vicious cases she (we) had ever become involved in, held at a neighboring town's Edgar Allan Poe festival (*Antiques Ravin'*); but her decidedly inventive – if sometimes illegal – methods of law enforcement did not sit well with the powers that be of the county seat. In fact, it got them off their seat and on their feet in indignation.

This morning, Mother was gone by the time I climbed out of bed, roused by Sushi, who wanted her breakfast; the little furball had long ago learned not to come too close to me while barking her wake-up call, else getting stuffed unceremoniously under the covers.

In the kitchen, a thoughtful Mother had set out a plate of baked waffles, which were still warm, so she must have just left. This made me smile, whether in response to the waffles or her absence, I leave for you to determine.

There was also a note saying she didn't know when she'd be back; nearby was her cell phone, which Mother never took with her when out 'investigating.' Or as I like to call it, 'stirring up trouble.'

This did not make me smile.

Well, actually it did, if a smirk counts as a smile. Because for once I wasn't worried about her shenanigans, as this time I would be on top of her whereabouts, having put a GPS tracker on the Vespa. I could summon the scooter's location with either my phone or the computer at the shop.

Cue the evil laugh.

And now cue a family recipe.

Waffles (Frasvafflor)

2 cups heavy sweet cream
1 and ⅓ cups sifted flour
4 tablespoons ice water
½ cup butter

Whip the cream stiff, whip in the flour, then the ice water.
Chill the batter in the fridge for one hour. When ready
to use, melt the butter and stir it into the batter. Heat a
waffle iron and spoon a little batter into each section.
Bake like any waffle. When browned, remove with a fork.
Sprinkle waffles with powdered sugar, and serve with
jam or fruit compote or whipped cream and almonds.
Makes enough crisp waffles for six servings.

Before continuing on with our story, I would like to take this
opportunity to address those who contacted me on Facebook,
Twitter, Instagram, WhatsApp, and snail mail, complaining
about the recipe I shared in *Antiques Bizarre*, for 'Mrs
Mulligan's Spicy Beef Stew.' I must point out that the recipe
was Mrs Mulligan's, not mine. And since the main beef (pun
intended) was its spiciness, the recipe *does* say spicy. When
the book goes into another printing, I will adjust the measure-
ment of cumin – or perhaps substitute mild chili powder for
hot – or maybe suggest an after-dinner antacid in place of
a mint.

After feeding Sushi and giving her an insulin shot, and
feeding myself, I took a quick shower, then threw on my
favorite skinny dark-washed jeans, a flowy floral shirt, and
designer flats that had been mismarked down, a fact I
neglected to point out to the shop. (Best you know at this
stage of the proceedings that I am not without flaws.) (Also,
that the one thing Mother and I have in common in our
writing styles is a use of parenthetical remarks that drives
some people crazy.)

(Sorry.)

Ready to face the world on a sunny spring morning, I
scooped up Sushi, made sure the house was locked, went out to

our recently purchased Ford Fusion, then headed downtown to open the shop.

Our antiques store, Trash 'n' Treasures, is located at the end of Main Street, in an old house at the base of West Hill, the area of town where all the lumber barons, pearl-button manufacturers, and bank founders had long ago built their mansions; the higher you climb, the grander they get, each trying to outdo the other.

Mother and I had been able to buy the somewhat-dilapidated two-story clapboard on the cheap, because during the 1950s an unsolved Lizzie Borden-type axe murder had taken place there. Over the years, an array of owners quickly fled, claiming the place was haunted. But the idea of ghosts didn't bother either of us. Anyway, Mother may well have scared the spooks off.

There *had* been a few strange occurrences when we'd first opened, like objects being moved from one room to another, and a rocking chair that, like Bruce Springsteen, just wouldn't stop rocking. Plus, once I felt a rush of cold air and thought someone brushed past me. But after Mother and I solved that long-ago murder – which had been related to a current, similar one (*Antiques Chop*) – we've had no bumps in the night (or day) since.

Of course life with Mother is always at least a little bumpy.

I parked in a spot behind the house, and we went in through the back, stepping into a mudroom lined with old crocks, then entered the kitchen, Sushi leading the way – like most dogs, Soosh never met a kitchen she didn't like.

Mother and I had decided to gear each room toward its original purpose – that is to say, all of our kitchen antiques were in the kitchen, bedroom sets in the bedrooms, linens in the linen closet, steamer trunks and old doors in the attic, formal furniture in the parlor, books in the library, and 'mantiques' like beer-signs and tools in the basement. Even the knickknacks were placed where you might expect them to be.

Often the wafting aroma of freshly baked chocolate chip cookies would lure patrons to the kitchen, where they were welcome to sit at the red-and-yellow boomerang-print laminated table and partake of the free goodies, along with a cup of strong coffee (no purchase of merchandise required).

Our customers often claimed that shopping at Trash 'n' Treasures gave them the vague sense of visiting an elderly relative – a grandmother, perhaps, or kindly old aunt. Only here, you didn't have to wait to inherit something; for the listed price (or maybe a haggled-over lower one), you could walk right out with whatever caught your eye.

The first thing I did was get the cookies baking and coffee going, before walking down the center hallway to the foyer, where we had installed a checkout counter. From a drawer, I selected two flags; one with my name, the other, Sushi's, which would be run up a pole attached to the front porch to tell customers who was in.

Mother had gotten the idea from Buckingham Palace, where a flag would fly when the Queen was in residence. Besides Mother, myself and Sushi, Joe Lange (a friend from my community college days who we employed part-time) also had one. When we were really busy, like at Christmastime, all four flags might be flapping. Other times, if Mother and I were off on a case, and Joe was having a PTSD attack from his tour in Iraq, nobody's flag was flying, meaning the shop was closed.

Then I settled in at the counter – I'd left Sushi in the kitchen, to sit staring at the oven as the cookies cooked – and turned on the computer, bringing up my GPS tracker app. The red teardrop on the map represented Mother, indicating she was currently at the Dunn Crematory, no doubt bothering poor grieving folks at some visitation or funeral.

After that, the morning got off to a slow, customer-free start, allowing me to work on the inventory spreadsheet; but then things began to pick up. Which was good, because we could use the income, what with a trip to London coming up – we had an as yet un-alienated editor to meet at our new publisher's.

For the next two hours, I was kept busy at the register – Sushi was busy, too, as she followed people around. Most of the customer flurry occurred in the kitchen, with purchases of old cast-iron skillets and bakeware, mid-century casserole dishes like Pyrex and Corningware, and jadite Fire King dishes.

Also, older cookbooks, before preparing meals got so fancy and time-consuming.

From the basement, I sold a large authentic Coca-Cola red round thermometer, a red-and-blue neon Standard Oil sign with flickering flame, and a wooden crate advertising Sky Ranch Washington apples, with an apple-headed cowboy getting ready to lasso another apple. (I don't explain such things, I just sell them.)

Upstairs, the bathroom medicine cabinet relinquished a silver double-edged men's razor, and an unopened pack of old double-edge blades; the 'teen' bedroom was cleared of a movie wall poster of *Ferris Bueller's Day Off*, along with a stack of vintage 70s LPs, which we had taken a chance on buying after learning vinyl records had become hot items.

I also got some real interest in a Heywood Wakefield bamboo bedroom set that Mother had cherry-picked from a motel that hadn't remodeled since back when everybody liked Ike . . . but the potential buyer would have to go home and talk to his wife about it. So I didn't expect to see him again.

Around noon the dust settled. In Serenity, the antiquing bug usually bites in the morning, then our buyers and browsers are off doing other things. I took a welcome cookie/coffee break at the counter – carefully breaking off bitty bites that did not include chocolate to share with Soosh – only to be interrupted by the arrival of Dumpster Dan.

Before you think I'm being derogatory, that title was given to Dan for and by himself, because his M.O. was scouring downtown dumpsters, looking for something, anything, he might be able to sell.

I gave him a cheery hello and a smile, and he shyly returned both, as if embarrassed to be alive. He had wispy white hair and glasses, the thick lenses reducing his eyes to the size of raisins, and was wearing his usual wrinkled khaki cargo pants and safari-type jacket, his world a concrete jungle.

I asked him, 'Still at the old Y?'

When a new YMCA was built, the old former building, with its many small rooms, was turned into a refuge for those who needed somewhere to stay until they got on their feet (mostly men), with a separate wing for others suffering from physical abuse (mostly women). A few folks, like Dan, have made Heart of Hearts, as the building was re-christened, their permanent home, paying whatever they could afford.

'Still there,' he said.

'Haven't seen you lately, Dan.'

'Been under the weather for a while.'

I frowned, concerned. 'All right, now?'

'Oh yes.'

Normally, Sushi, who had retired to her bed on the floor behind me, would have come out to greet Dan and his tantalizing (to her) bouquet. But apparently she was too pooped – dogging customers around can take it out of a girl.

'Got something for me?' I asked, which was usually the reason for his visit.

And whatever he had, which was typically not worth much, we had a policy of taking, to help him out.

(Early on, Dan had once brought in an inexpensive figurine that had been glued back together. I bought it, then tossed it in a dumpster a few blocks away. A few days later, he brought the same figurine back. 'Here's another one of those you seemed to like so much. Now you'll have a pair!')

'I got a box of books,' he said, a thumb over his shoulder, 'out on the porch.'

Internally, I groaned. Books were bad sellers for us, took up needed space, and the library room shelves were already packed full.

Still, I had Dan haul them in, bought the books for probably more than I should (a few old cheap-edition mysteries might appeal to Mother for her own collection), and stuck the box beneath the counter.

No sooner had he left when the bell above the front door jingled again.

'Hi, Beautiful,' said the chief of the Serenity Police Department. When he said that, as he often did, he sounded like Paul Drake greeting Della Street in those old *Perry Mason* shows that Mother so loves to watch.

Tony – in his late forties with graying temples, steel-gray eyes, bulbous nose, square jaw, thick neck and barrel chest – was just about anybody's idea of a man's man. He was wearing his usual office attire – light blue shirt (sleeves rolled back), navy tie, gray slacks (badge attached to brown belt), and brown Florsheim shoes.

In addition to being police chief, he was my fiancé, a status he'd assumed recently – getting engaged was a step we'd taken after Mother stepped down as sheriff, thinking (perhaps optimistically) that life might become calmer.

When I first arrived back in Serenity, Tony and I mixed like oil and water – mostly over Mother's interference in police matters. But, you know what happens if you keep stirring . . . the oil and water blend pretty well.

Now, for *this* guest, Sushi dislodged herself from the bed, and came around the counter to paw eagerly at Tony's legs – partially because she liked Tony, but mostly because she *really* liked his dog, Rocky, and could catch a scent of him.

Tony scratched Soosh's furry head – it took a while, but finally, satisfied, she trotted contentedly back to her bunker.

'Care for some coffee?' I asked. 'I think we have a few cookies left.'

'No thanks.' He strode forward. 'Ready for London?'

'Noooo,' I said, and sighed. 'I'm afraid it's going to bankrupt us.'

'Oh?'

I nodded. 'Mother insisted we fly First Class and stay at the Savoy.'

'She could go alone. You don't *both* have to meet your editor.'

I made a face. 'Do you know what kind of trouble Mother could get into, left to her own devices?'

His eyebrows went up. 'Point well taken.'

'As a matter of fact,' I said, my eyebrows going up as his came down, 'I think you should call Scotland Yard and warn them she's coming.'

'Good idea.'

'I'm serious, Tony.'

'Oh, so am I.'

'Speaking of Mother,' I said, looking at the computer screen, 'I'd better see where she is right now.'

Tony came around the counter wearing a thoughtful frown. 'You're tracking her again? After what happened the last time?'

Mother had left the GPS device on the trolley-bus where, a while back, I'd previously tried to follow her path.

I said, 'She would never expect it.'

Tony snorted a laugh. 'Don't count on that.'

'Have a little faith in me. If by this point I can't outsmart her, I should just give up.' I refreshed the map on the screen, where the red teardrop was moving south on highway 218.

'What the . . .?' I said. 'What's she doing heading toward *Missouri*?'

Tony leaned in, frowning. 'And doing a pretty good clip at that.'

'How fast can a Vespa go, anyway?' I asked.

His eyebrows went up again. 'Sixty maybe – some, even eighty.'

'Are they *legal* on the highway?'

A one-shoulder shrug. 'Technically, yes . . . but I wouldn't recommend it.'

I could feel my Prozac being tested. 'Well, what can I *do*?'

'Call her cell,' Tony suggested.

I gave him a disparaging look.

'Oh, right,' he said. 'She never takes it with her when she's "investigating."' A startled expression. '*What* is she investigating?'

'No idea,' I said. 'She hasn't mentioned anything, except frustration over us not having anything to write about right now. It must be some potential case she found out about this morning.'

His eyes were wide. 'I don't know of any murders. What, is she ahead of *me* now?'

'You said it, not me.'

'Are you implying she wants a murder investigation in her pocket when you meet with your new publisher?'

'What do you think?'

Tony touched his forehead as if taking his own temperature. 'You don't want to know.'

'Is there anything you can do to stop her?' I pleaded.

'She's going to be over the Iowa/Missouri border before too long!'

He stepped back, got his cell from pants pocket, and speed-dialed. 'Rosa . . . have Ron Kaufman at State Patrol call me ASAP.'

He ended the call and asked me, 'What app are you using, and what's your password?'

I wrote the information down quickly on a scrap of paper, and handed it to him.

He asked, 'And there's only one tracker on the screen?'

'Yes.'

Tony's cell sounded, an old-fashioned phone ring, and he moved around the counter, then toward the front door, so I only got his side of the conversation.

'Yeah, Ron. Have someone stop a Vespa on 218 about thirty, forty miles from Missouri . . . yes, Vespa. No, there's no BOLO – her daughter is concerned. Woman in question is Vivian Borne. Not dangerous. But could be off her rocker. Right. Thanks.'

He gave the tracker information, then returned the cell to his pocket.

I arched an eyebrow. 'Off her rocker?'

He shrugged. 'Isn't that what you're thinking?'

'Yes, but *off her rocker*? Didn't your police training on mental illness teach you anything?'

He spread his hands. 'I said she wasn't dangerous.'

'She might be to herself.' My eyes drifted to the screen. 'Tony! She's stopped at a restaurant in Donnellson.'

He looked. 'They'll be able to see that, thanks to your app. Buy us some time if she has lunch.'

'So we just have to wait,' I sighed.

Not wanting to deal with customers, I went outside and retrieved the two flags, indicating the shop was closed to regular customers, but left the front door unlocked.

I had just rejoined Tony at the computer, when the red marker suddenly began to move, fast, heading through the tiny town on Burlington Street and into farmland.

'She's trying to flee!' I said, glued to the screen.

On a tight curve, the marker left the road, then stopped abruptly, in what I could only assume was a ditch.

'Oh, Tony!' I grabbed his arm.

A Trash 'n' Treasures Tip

Predicting trends can be difficult for antiques dealers, so paying attention to lifestyle changes is important. For example, with the arrival of the 'man cave' came an immediate need to fill it. Nowadays, both Millennials, starting out in smaller spaces, and Boomers, exchanging larger dwellings for condos, find little interest in buying bulky antiques. Which means a lot of time for me spent dusting that huge Victorian coatrack at the shop.

TWO
Carry On Regardless

Vivian back at the helm, you lucky people!

Earlier that morning, dressed in black slacks and a lavender sweater set, I was tooling along budding, tree-lined Mulberry Avenue on my almost-new mint-green Vespa, just like the motorbike Audrey Hepburn rode in the movie *Roman Holiday*, and feeling very much like the actress herself. That is, as if I were slender, twenty-four, had long dark hair, and Gregory Peck was alive, well, and interested.

My first stop would be Dunn Cremation and Burial, a modern facility on the edge of town, where I've made my own final resting plans (not trusting Brandy to give me a properly showy send-off).

The parking lot was packed, the ol' grim reaper working overtime, but nonetheless I found a spot for the Vespa, dismounted, smoothed my hair, and checked my teeth for bugs. Then I searched the motorbike from nose to tail (sticking with the horse analogy) to locate any GPS disc that Brandy might have hidden somewhere to keep tabs on me via our store's computer app. Did she think I was born yesterday? Never mind *how* many yesterdays . . .

The ungrateful child had tracked me once before when I'd taken the free trolley-converted-to-gas downtown to do a little investigating on my own. But the foolish girl had left my AARP magazine in our (shall we say) reading room, folded open to the ad for the device. And I'd found the small, round GPS button without difficulty, sewn (badly) into the lining of my coat, which I then removed (the button, not the coat) and left under my trolley bus seat, where it went round and round the town (the button, not the seat or the trolley, although they did, as well).

Are we clear?

On this fine spring morn, Brandy had taped the device beneath the back bumper. But I left it there for the nonce. Why not let her think she was on top of things?

I entered the facility through two sets of double glass doors and into a large, tastefully appointed greeting area, off of which four individual, mourner-occupied rooms flowed.

'May I help you?' asked a woman of perhaps forty, appropriately somber in both attire and expression. I had not seen her here before.

The woman went on, 'Are you attending the Lewis, Morton, Phillips, or Stevens visitation?' Thoughtful of her to put them in non-preferential alphabetical order. As a Borne, when my time came, there was a good chance I'd be first.

'*Which* Stevens?' I asked.

'Mildred.'

'Oh dear. When did this happen?'

'Two days ago.'

My eyebrows went up. 'I hadn't heard . . . I must be slipping. Goodness gracious, past the century mark – I thought she'd never go!' I paused. 'Dear, an open mouth is not a good look on anyone, much less a greeter. Actually I'm not here for a visitation, rather to consult with Mr Dunn.'

She stiffened (no pun intended). 'I'm afraid he's terribly busy at the moment. Perhaps . . .'

'It's all right, Laura,' said the owner of the facility, who'd come up behind her.

Mid-sixties, impeccably dressed in a dark gray pin-striped suit, white hair parted perfectly on one side, Ned Dunn had once asked me to marry him, six months or so after his wife passed on. He's nice enough, and his business was always booming (thanks to aging Boomers), but I had no desire to get stuck out front being a traffic cop to the grieving like Laura.

Who he was telling, 'Vivian Borne can see me any time.'

The woman backed away, looking confused for some reason, and I followed Ned into his office, which had a curtained window, open at the moment onto the lobby area.

The room was pleasantly decorated – not too flashy, to prevent any thoughts of him overcharging, and with just the

right warm-wood trappings to create a vague, non-denomin-
ational religious ambiance.

He gestured to a comfortable chair, then took his seat behind
the clutter-free desk.

When we'd settled, I said, 'I see the new roof is finished.'

Ned nodded. 'A metal one with a lifetime guarantee, so I'll
never have to replace it again.'

Not in the rest of *his* lifetime, anyway.

Getting around to the purpose of my visit, I asked, 'Anything
for me?'

'Nothing suspicious, I'm afraid, Vivian,' he replied. 'Mr
Lewis had a fatal heart attack . . .'

'After hitting a hole in one, I heard. Do hope he had time
to enjoy it even for a moment.'

'Mrs Morton died in a single car accident . . .'

'Ten'll get you twenty she wasn't wearing her glasses.'

'Mr Phillips died after a lengthy illness . . .'

'At least he had time to get his affairs in order – financial
and private.'

'And Mrs Stevens from old age.'

'Well, one-hundred-and-one! She was asking for it.'

A long pause. His expression reminded me of that poor
squirrel's right before Brandy couldn't avoid running it down.

'Just a little jest,' I said, 'courtesy of Mel Brooks. Honestly,
Ned, what's wrong with a little levity to liven up the joint?'

Ned had no answer for that, but then it was a rhetorical
question, wasn't it? He cleared his throat. 'Anyway, Vivian,
nothing seems overtly suspicious about any of these
passings.'

I sighed. 'Well, thank you, Ned. I won't take up any more
of your time.'

I started to stand, but then froze in place.

'"Overtly?"'

'Well, no, not really. It's just . . .'

I plopped back down. 'Just *what*, Ned? You know everything
you tell me stays between us. What happens at the funeral
parlor stays at the funeral parlor.'

The man sat forward, elbows on the desk, tenting his hands.
'Do you recall, about a month ago, Ruth Hassler broke her

neck, falling down the stairs? Friend of yours, wasn't she? Her services were here, but I don't believe you attended.'

I nodded. 'I'd meant to, but was tied up with that Wentworth fire investigation.' (*Antiques Fire Sale.*)

When Ned didn't continue, I gestured. 'And?'

'Well, during visitation, I overheard a few whispers.'

Another irritating pause. '*About?* I'm growing moss here, Ned.'

'About why she hadn't used her stair-lift.'

Interesting.

'I suppose she was cremated?'

He nodded.

'So there's no need for a backhoe,' I grumbled.

I just *loved* it when Perry Mason (Raymond Burr on the vintage TV show) would get a court order for an exhumation!

I lamented, 'Honestly, this trend toward cremation is causing me problems!'

Ned shrugged. 'Not much I can do about it.'

'Have you tried running a special on embalming? A BOGO sale maybe?'

A knock at the door. It opened and Laura stuck her head in.

'I'm sorry to disturb you, Mr Dunn, but you're needed.'

'That's fine,' he said. 'Mrs Borne and I were finished.'

I rose and said cheerfully, 'Don't say "finished," Ned – coming from a funeral director, it's a tad unsettling!'

After Ned departed with his greeter, who was white as a ghost for some reason, I lingered for a few moments, digesting what he'd said, then left.

At my Vespa in the parking lot, I removed the GPS button, and, while pretending to tie my Nikes, stuck the device under the chassis of the car parked next to me.

My next stop was to consult with Zelda, a new informant of mine who was proving most valuable. I'd set the meeting at our usual place, Cinders, a bar located on Main Street in one of the many boxcar-style Victorian brick buildings lining the five-block business district.

Renny, latest owner of this enduring if eccentric watering

hole, had been for years an enthusiastic buyer of eclectic collectibles, filling her establishment with hundreds of pop-culture castaways, all available for sale, although nothing was marked. If a patron saw something he or she liked, an offer was made, which Renny might or might not accept, depending upon her whim and current cash flow.

Seeing someone who'd gotten a little tipsy departing Cinders with a collectible was not an unusual occurrence – a life-size standee of Mr Spock tucked under an arm, perhaps, or a *Star Wars* lightsaber in one hand, or maybe the famous 1970s poster of Farrah Fawcett on a skateboard, rolled into a tube (the poster, not Farrah) (or the skateboard either, for that matter).

Without knowing it, or perhaps sensing a coming trend, Renny had, in years of largely indiscriminate collecting, made the bar a real draw for the local hipster crowd – twenty- and thirty-somethings who loved to hang out there, as well as a lovable assortment of oddballs who were welcome as long as they behaved themselves.

Inside the entrance at left was a huge, completely furnished dollhouse, as well as a vast collection of Elvis memorabilia. Continuing along the left-hand wall was a long bar with a dozen red-vinyl bucket-seats, a row of lava lamps providing more mood than lighting.

Hugging the right wall, and nearly as long as the counter, was a shuffleboard game with little tables and chairs to one side for players to keep score. Following this came a 1950s jukebox, then a rather impressive collection of Marilyn Monroe and Betty Boop collectibles, all basking in the glow of hundreds upon hundreds of twinkle lights of varied colors strung everywhere.

And that is but an example of the first of four rooms leading back to an alley. The second was an homage to the '80s; third, a Mexican cantina; fourth, a tropical oasis, where fake palm trees were home to stuffed monkeys (she used to have a stuffed camel as well, under the tree, but the Dromedary took up too much space and kept falling over).

Renny, polishing glasses behind the bar, smiled upon seeing me. 'Hello, Vivian. Your usual?'

In her early fifties with a bubbly personality, Renny sported long blonde hair, pretty features, a curvaceous figure, and a preference for leopard-print attire.

'Set me up!' I said. Never too early in the day for my drink of preference: a Shirley Temple. And no one out-mixed Renny in assembling just the right combination of lemon-lime soda and grenadine syrup, or her generosity in adding extra Maraschino cherries.

Non-alcoholic beverages had been my preference for some years now, ever since I'd made the mistake of partaking of a glass of wine while on my bi-polar medication, then boarding a Greyhound bus where I ended up in Poughkeepsie.

Seated at the end of the bar was Nona, a close friend of Zelda's and the entity I had to go through to contact my informant. One might say the two were inseparable.

I strolled over to the slender woman. In her mid-twenties with a narrow face, thin lips, and long dark hair, Nona wore purple-framed glasses, an oversize brown leather bomber jacket, short red-and-tan plaid skirt, ripped black tights, and floral combat boots. In earlier times, one might have called Nona a beatnik.

'And how are you doing this fine morning, my dear?' I asked chirpily.

'OK, I guess,' she replied, not sounding at all OK, one hand on the stem of a nearly empty glass of red wine.

I nodded to the vacant chair next to Nona, where an untouched tumbler of whiskey sat before it. 'And Zelda? How is she?'

Now might be a good time to tell you, dear reader, that Zelda apparently exists only in the imagination of Nona, who is a tulpamancer, or 'tulpa' for short. Tulpamancy is considered a mental condition in which a person will summon an imaginary companion, not unlike a child who may go through an 'invisible friend' phase. For tulpas, however, the attachments do not disappear with age, but only grow stronger.

Little is known about tulpamancy – which might indeed be a form of mental illness, although some see it as a manifestation of the paranormal. Taken as a whole, these imaginary friends have a positive influence, and the voices that tulpas hear in their heads from these attachments are nothing like the ones I hear when I go off my medication. You don't even want to know!

To my query of how Zelda was feeling today, Nona snapped, 'Why don't you ask *her*? She's sitting right there!'

(In my defense, sometimes I would address an empty chair only to be informed that Zelda was in the ladies' room.)

I sensed something was wrong between the pair.

'Are you girls having a little tiff?' I asked Nona gently.

'More than a little,' she responded glumly.

I hoisted myself up into the chair next to Zelda's and looked down the bar and asked, 'What seems to be the problem?'

Nona stared into her glass of wine. 'She . . . she wants her freedom.'

'Oh, dear,' I blurted. 'We can't have that!'

So far Zelda was batting one thousand on her tips. And I just couldn't face breaking in a new informant. (Granted, an imaginary friend might not make a terribly good eyewitness, especially if called upon to testify.)

I backtracked. 'What I mean is . . . it would be a shame to end the friendship. Doesn't Zelda go off on her own sometimes?'

'Yes,' Nona admitted.

'Then why not give her a little more freedom?'

Her voice cracked. 'I'm afraid . . . afraid she'll find someone else.'

'Nonsense,' I scoffed. 'Let me speak to her.'

Nona thought about that. 'Do you think it would help?'

'Couldn't hurt. Why don't you take a trip back to the '80s, so we can have some privacy.'

She nodded, slid out of the chair, and disappeared through a beaded curtain into the next room.

While I didn't exactly believe that Zelda really existed, I saw no harm in speaking to the empty seat. 'Look, young lady – I need you, and Nona needs you, and you'll never find a better, more loyal friend.'

I didn't really have anything else to say to Zelda, but I didn't want to summon Nona back so early that it might seem

I hadn't made a good effort on the tulpa's behalf. So I recited Shakespeare's speech from *Hamlet*, 'To be or not to be, that is the question. Whether 'tis nobler,' yada yada yada.

When I had finished, I called out to Nona to return, which she did, then I moved to the other end of the bar for some small talk with Renny, so the two friends could (hopefully) make up.

After a few minutes, when Nona began to smile, her spirits apparently lifted, I returned to the seat next to Zelda.

'Everything hunky-dory?' I asked.

Nona said, almost sheepishly, 'Yes. We've decided that Zelda can go off by herself, from time to time, and in return, she'll let me know when, rather than just, you know . . . vanishing. I mean, imagine it, Vivian – what if you were talking to someone who suddenly wasn't there?'

'That would be a kick in the slats,' I admitted. 'But you seem to've resolved this in a most fair fashion. Might Zelda and I conduct some business, dear?'

Since my informant's responses had to come through Nona, I looked at her, not the invisible Zelda.

'She says that would be fine,' Nona replied.

Back to Zelda. 'Do you have any leads for me?'

Sometimes this process could take a while, especially if Zelda had important information to impart, so I returned my attention to my Shirley Temple, which had thus far been neglected.

But, quite soon, Nona reported, 'She doesn't have anything.'

I raised my eyebrows. 'Nothing at *all*? Not even a whiff of malfeasance? It doesn't *have* to be a murder – although I would prefer it. Still, any nice juicy crime would do . . .'

Nona shrugged. 'Sorry. She says it's been very quiet out there.'

I grunted. '*Too quiet!* What am I going to tell my new publisher? They're going to expect a humdinger of a first book.' I paused, recalling my conversation with Ned. 'Zelda, what about Ruth Hassler? She fell down her stairs last month and broke her neck.'

After a full minute (which made me hopeful), Nona said, 'All Zelda knows is that Ruth's daughter and son-in-law, who live in town, inherited her estate. And they haven't been shy about spending money lately.'

I was the glum one now. 'Well, at least that's something to look in to. Thank you, Zelda. And let me know if you hear anything else about those free-spending relatives.'

I placed a fivespot on the counter and clambered out of the bucket seat. Waving goodbye to Renny, I was heading for the door when Nona caught up to me.

'Vivian, both Zelda and I want to thank you for, well, helping patch things up between us.'

I patted her arm. 'You're most welcome. But I'm sure you two would have arrived at the same understanding. I can't imagine anything coming between two people who are so closely intertwined.'

I turned away from Nona and was about to go out the door when she addressed my back, 'Oh! And Zelda wants you to know that your oration of Hamlet's speech was the second best she'd ever heard . . . right after Larry Olivier on TCM.'

I looked wide-eyed over at Renny, who shrugged, and said, 'She did seem to enjoy it.'

Outside, on the sidewalk, I was pondering my next move when I spotted Skylar James across the street, lounging in the doorway of his antiques store, The Trading Post. He summoned me with a smile and backward wave.

Leaving my Vespa in front of Cinders, I jaywalked over to the muscular young man, who was blessed with sandy hair, rugged good looks, and a pleasant cowboy vibe in his fringed suede jacket, plaid shirt, blue jeans and boots. Perhaps Brandy's age, he had moved here from New Mexico last year with his wife, a dark-haired filly with family ties in Serenity.

'And how is Angela?' I asked. She was a fourth-grade teacher, which might explain why they so far had no children.

'Always seems to have a darn cold,' he said with an easy grin, and slight western drawl. 'Comes with the job, I guess.'

'The little rascals are walking Petri dishes,' I said. Then, 'What can I do for you, Skylar?'

'Step into my parlor,' he said, and led me in.

As one might expect, The Trading Post's interior was rustic, with an original turn-of-last-century's wooden floor, brick walls, and high tin ceiling. Skylar's merchandise was mostly western Americana – silver and turquoise jewelry, Indian artifacts – plus 1940s and '50s TV and movie cowboy memorabilia, from Roy Rogers lunch boxes to framed movie posters of John Wayne in *Rio Bravo*.

Skylar asked, 'I was wonderin' if you'd do me a favor?'

We were standing near a display of western hats.

'Of course,' I said, adding, 'If I'm able,' leaving myself an out.

'I hear you're goin' to London soon.'

'That's right,' I said. Word does get around our little town – especially when it's spread my me.

'Well, Miz Borne . . .' He hesitated. 'This is a little embarrassin'. . .'

'I don't embarrass easily.'

'I sold one of my turquoise necklaces to the owner of a store there called the Old Curiosity Shop, by e-mail, and, well . . .'

'He expects you to cover the added expense of customs, and duty and VAT.'

Skylar nodded sheepishly. 'Not that it's a terribly expensive item, really – worth about two hundred – but with the added expense, I wouldn't make a darn thing.'

It had been a rough winter for antiques dealers, and knowing his wife was on a teacher's salary, I felt compelled to help this new member of the antiques community. But not compelled enough to break any laws, domestic or foreign. After all, I'm a former sheriff!

'Tell you what,' I said. 'You sell it to me now for the amount settled upon, and I'll sell it to the owner of the Old Curiosity Shop for that amount.'

Skylar smiled. 'And, if the Old Curiosity Shop dude doesn't like it, for some reason, or has changed his mind . . . I'll buy it right back on your return.'

'Fair enough,' I replied.

He stuck out a hand, which I shook. 'Thanks, Vivian. And if there's anythin' I can ever do for you, one antiquer to another . . . let me know.'

'Oh, just forget about that,' I said. But *I* wouldn't – I always call in my markers.

He stepped behind the glass display case of jewelry, unlocked a sliding door, and selected a silver necklace set with turquoise stones. Nothing terribly special perhaps, but certainly attractive.

I fastened it around my neck. Then I paid the two hundred, got a receipt, and Skylar gave me written information where to go once I got to London.

Back on my Vespa across the street, I gazed in the side mirror at the necklace, sparkling and vibrant in the sun; it went perfectly with my outfit.

If the UK recipient reneged, I just might keep it.

Brandy back. Is everyone all right? Need a break? Perhaps some aspirin? At this point in our narrative, I had just clutched Tony's arm, alarmed by the GPS app's indication that Mother seemed to have veered off into a ditch near the Missouri border.

The bell over the front door tinkled – apparently some customer who didn't know our flag routine. Why hadn't I simply locked the door?

'Hello, you two!' Mother said. 'Slow day?'

I picked up the nearest thing on the counter – a tennis ball I squeeze for stress relief – and threw it at her, and she caught it like a line drive.

'Such violence,' she tsk-tsked, 'and in front of our police chief!'

Several minutes later, Mother and I were seated in the kitchen, at the red-and-yellow laminated table. Tony was out in the foyer, on his cell, explaining to Ron at the State Police that Mother was safely back on her rocker.

Mother, pretending to pout, said, 'You could have hit me with that dreadful ball.'

'I wish I had. Might've knocked some sense into you.'

Since the pouting hadn't worked, she turned defensive. '*You* started this, utilizing those high-tech devices.'

I waggled a finger. 'Leaving one on a bus was bad enough . . . but on an out-of-state car? Do you know how worried I was? Enough to involve Tony!'

Mother spread her hands. 'Dear, I had no idea the car I utilized was going to Missouri. It just happened to be the one next to me in the lot.'

Tony entered the room, his expression unreadable.

I asked, 'How much trouble did the Borne girls make for you?'

He walked over to the coffee pot, poured himself a cup, then pulled out a chair next to me.

'Not much,' he admitted, adding, 'I may even receive a commendation.'

'For *what*?' Mother and I asked together.

He drank from the cup. 'For helping catch one of the most wanted men in the Midwest. Bank robber.'

While I grappled with that, Mother said cheerfully, 'Well, there you go! Win-win!'

I glared at her. 'And how is that the case?'

'*You* have finally learned not to bug your mother – electronically and otherwise – and the *chief* receives a much-deserved accolade.' She looked across at Tony. 'What do you suppose this miscreant was doing at the funeral home?'

'Boosting a vehicle,' Tony said. 'He left a stolen car behind and took one belonging to a mourner attending a visitation.'

Mother commented, 'Which happened to be the car I put the GPS gizmo under.' She chuckled. 'I solve crimes without even trying! Do you think there might be some recognition for *me*, as well? After all, I did set this whole exciting chain of events in motion.'

Tony merely stared at her with those steel-gray eyes.

'Maybe a little squib in the *Serenity Sentinel*?' she pressed.

The chief downed the rest of his coffee, and pushed back his chair.

Mother's eyes followed him as he stood. 'How about a hardy hand-shake?'

As Tony left the kitchen, she called out, 'Just knowing I helped will be quite enough!'

The front door slammed.

She turned to me. 'Perhaps you could leak something to the radio station.'

'Don't push it.'

Mother sighed, reached for a cookie on the platter in front of us, and took a big bite.

'Well, no matter,' she said, chewing absent-mindedly. 'I'm sure the Fourth Estate will find out somehow.'

So was I.

Moving to a less contentious topic, I asked, 'What's that around your neck?'

She looked down at the necklace. 'Lovely isn't it?'

'I don't remember ever seeing you wear anything like that,' I commented. 'But it *is* attractive. The turquoise brings out the color of your eyes.'

'Why, thank you, dear. I bought it at The Trading Post.'

'Haven't been in there yet.'

'Nice store, if you like western Americana.'

'Any furniture?'

'A few Victorian pieces,' she said, then sniffed. 'But a little too *bordello* for my taste.'

On friendlier footing now, I gave Mother a rundown of what had sold this morning, which further improved the atmosphere.

'Well, that just about pays for the hotel!' she said, beaming. 'I do hope something good is playing at the Savoy Theatre. Did I ever tell you about the time I performed there with Elaine Stritch back in '63?'

'You *did*?'

'Don't look so surprised, dear. I wasn't *always* relegated to community theater.' She continued: 'Granted, it was a small part . . . what you might call a walk-on . . . in Noel Coward's *Sail Away*. You see, during the second act, I was looking for the loo, found myself backstage, and took a wrong turn.'

My eyes widened. 'Onto the stage?'

Mother nodded. 'But fleet of foot and thought, I merely pretended to be just another annoying passenger on the boat.'

No experience necessary.

'So when you say it was a "walk-on" part,' I said, 'you mean you just walked on.'

Mother ignored that. 'Elaine was quite nice about it – in fact, she invited me to stay for the curtain call.' Mother put a finger to her lips. 'I wonder if the theater still has those geranium-hued seats. If so, we must find out *what* color they are now, so you and I can coordinate our outfits. Don't want to disappear into our chairs!'

Wishing I could disappear right now, I said, 'Let's go home.'

I was shutting down the computer when I remembered to tell Mother about the box Dan had brought in.

'I thought we had agreed to a moratorium on buying any further books,' Mother said. 'The shelves are over-stuffed as it is. Any more will ruin the bindings.'

'I know . . . but there *are* a few vintage mysteries.'

'That's some solace, dear. Anyway, I would have done the same for darling Dan. Well, we'll stick the box in the trunk and lug them home. We may find a few worth keeping.'

While Mother locked up, I went out to the Fusion with the box, a reinvigorated Sushi trotting behind.

Driving home, I asked archly, 'Anything you care to share with me about *your* morning?'

'Quite uneventful compared to yours, dear,' she commented. 'But I will say that I might have a lead on something for the upcoming book.'

She told me about Ruth Hassler, an elderly widow who'd fallen down the stairs to her death, even though she usually used a stair-lift.

'Sounds a little thin,' I said.

'I think it has possibilities,' she countered.

'Let's face it, Mother – we may have run out of murders to solve. We might actually have to *make up* a mystery.'

'What! Never! Did John Watson ever stray from the truth in chronicling the cases of Sherlock Holmes? Did Archie Goodwin ever make up a story about Nero Wolfe? Would Arthur Hastings ever tell a fib about Hercule Poirot? No siree. To do otherwise would be heresy!'

Sorry, but as I've explained before, once you get on, you can't get off the express. And neither can I.

Even if one of us pulls the emergency cord.

A Trash 'n' Treasures Tip

When exporting items abroad, take into consideration the cost of that country's import charges. It may not be worth the effort. Unless you have a dodgy friend heading to the locale.

THREE
Carry On England

With my friend Joe running the store, and Tony taking Sushi (who was thrilled to be with Rocky), Mother and I boarded a puddle-jumper at the Serenity Municipal Airport for Chicago, to catch an overnight flight to London.

Mother had insisted on British Airways, the Airbus 380 – a decision that nearly decimated our bank account – booking two First Class seats through something called World Club.

After clearing security at O'Hare – Mother'd had her recent passport photo taken three times at Walgreens before one met her approval – we were soon herded onto the massive double-decker jet, greeted by a female flight attendant with a pleasant British accent, crisp white blouse, navy skirt and sensible pumps. Our seats were on the upper level, via a front flight of stairs, and we found our places on an aisle and window. We were enclosed, capsule-like, for privacy.

Now this was the way to fly!

Taking the one by the window, knowing from past experience that Mother would have to relieve herself more often than me, I settled into the cubbyhole and began familiarizing myself with what would be my little world for the next nine hours.

Through a separating partition that (we'd been told) couldn't be closed until airborne, Mother said, 'I was just visiting with such a *nice* young man in the waiting area. His name is Andrew.'

'Uh-huh,' I said, continuing to check out my world – pillow, blanket, headphones, cloth bag with amenities, including eye mask, toothbrush and paste, and skin cream . . .

'And he showed me a picture of his lovely wife and two adorable little children.'

'That's nice.' Pop-out TV screen, entertainment control panel, seat and panel controls . . .

'He's been on a furlough to see them, and is on his way back to Iraq.'

'Dirty job, but somebody's got to do it, I guess.' Power adapter, side storage bins, fold-down ottoman to make a bed . . . wait a minute.

Get in the game, Brandy! This is no idle chit-chat from Mother, passing the time till take-off.

'Poor darling,' she was saying. 'He's six-foot-four, and simply *stuffed* into a seat on the lower level in coach.'

I viewed her through narrowed eyes. 'You haven't offered him *my* seat, by any chance?'

'I knew you'd understand, dear!'

I sat up, as if thrust forward by turbulence, though the plane was on the ground. 'No, I *don't* understand! What's wrong with offering him *your* seat, if you're such a passionate patriot?'

She put a finger to her lips. 'I *did* consider it. But that would be quite impossible considering my double hip replacements, lumbago, arthritis, and plantar fasciculus.'

'You left out hammer toes.'

'Well, I didn't want to sound like a complainer.'

I whined, 'But I've never *flown* this *nice* before!'

'I'm sure you'll have plenty of opportunities to do so in the future . . . but that brave soldier may not.' A dramatic beat. 'Dear, his job is disposing of explosives. As you say, a dirty job but someone has to do it.'

Fuming, I snapped, 'Oh, fine.'

Mother reached through the opening and patted my hand. 'Good girl! I knew you'd do the right thing, so I've already made the arrangements and asked a flight attendant to show him up.'

The young veteran who arrived was indeed tall, and muscular, and, yes, would have suffered an extremely uncomfortable flight. Giving up one of our seats was a dirty job, but . . .

I gathered my things, then on my way into the aisle, purposely stepped on Mother's foot, and she howled as if she'd spotted a gremlin on the wing of the plane.

'This is awfully nice of you,' Andrew addressed me. 'But are you sure?'

I gave him a smile I hoped looked sincere. 'Happy to do it.'

'Well, I can't thank you enough.'

As we exchanged tickets, I commented, 'There are earplugs in the little bag – she snores.'

'That's a scurrilous accusation,' Mother grumbled, rubbing her foot.

'And a true one,' I whispered, and the soldier smiled.

After taking the back stairs to the lower coach section, I located my seat in the center of a middle row of five near the back of the plane. I managed not to bust out crying.

But as passengers struggled to their feet to let me in, a smattering of applause greeted me, as the soldier's former neighbors understood the sacrifice I'd made, which I didn't deserve since I'd been forced into it. I acknowledged this with a brave nod. Might as well take the credit.

An hour into the flight, dinner was served, but instead of the usual coach fare served to my neighbors, I was handed a large tray with nice tableware, the flight attendant saying, 'Compliments of British Airways.'

On a linen cloth was a fresh fruit salad, chicken-and-barley soup, filet of salmon, steamed vegetables, and for dessert, a divine-looking chocolate cake with vanilla pudding. Everything was scrumptious.

Later, when trays had been cleared, and the cabin lights dimmed, I fell asleep, and didn't wake up until breakfast. My meal, again, was First Class.

After a smooth landing at about nine in the morning London time, Mother was waiting for me inside Terminal Five, my group being the last to deplane.

'Well, dear, how was the flight?' she asked.

'I'm here,' I said stiffly, not mentioning the excellent food, how nice everyone was around me, and that I'd slept most of the way – that all in all I'd had a delightful flight. Let her think I suffered.

She was saying, 'Andrew wanted to tell you again how grateful he was, but he had a tight connection.' She paused.

'We did exchange information, so you'll probably be hearing from him.'

Little did the Iraq veteran know the price that seat upgrade would cost him. Mother would add him to her ever-growing Christmas letter list – where life-long friends and casual acquaintances received equal footing – off of which the only escape was via the grim reaper. (If you moved, she would only track you down.)

I took a moment to text Tony that we'd arrived, not expecting to hear back until later, since it was about three in the morning at home; but he responded immediately, saying he missed me, and adding that Sushi was curled up with Rocky.

After a trek to baggage claim – did you ever notice that the first luggage down the shoot at the carousel never belongs to anyone, and just goes around and around and around? – I was bracing for a long wait through processing. But Heathrow had installed e-gates for speedy entry for certain countries, which now included the USA: step up to a machine, insert your passport open to your photo, look into a screen, the machine makes a match, then off you go.

Only, there was a hitch with Mother. Remember how I said she'd had three different photos taken, before accepting the last one? That's because she went home and used a facial kit where rubber bands were attached in the hair, pulling back her skin – instant face-lift, an old (double meaning) Bette Davis trick.

An officious type came over and, as the British say, sorted things, after Mother reluctantly explained her recent youthful photo – 'I'm an actress, dear, and it's a technique we thespians use' – and we were sent on our way.

Not until I was settling back in one of those iconic black taxis could I finally relax, even if it was unnerving to see the driver – a pleasant-looking middle-aged chap in a sporty cap – seated on the right, as we traveled on the left.

The trip to the Savoy in Central London took about an hour, but that passed quickly as we gawked at such landmarks as the Victoria and Albert Museum, Harrods, and Trafalgar Square. Gliding by Buckingham Palace, where the Queen's flag was not flying today, Mother blurted, disappointedly, 'Oh, the old darling's not in,' as if we'd been planning to drop by for tea.

Through a hole in the Plexiglas separating us from the driver, he said, 'No, ma'am. The Queen 'ardly lives there anymore, preferring Windsor Castle.'

Soon the cab turned down a short, narrow street that ended in a circle with a fountain, beneath a grand overhang with the famously recognizable S A V O Y green neon sign.

Before we left Serenity, Mother had our banker get us British currency, to avoid the high airport exchange fees, and now she seemed to relish using some of the colorful bills to pay the driver and then tip the formally attired top-hatted doorman, who dealt with our luggage.

We whisked through one of two gleaming wood-and-glass revolving doors and stood agog, blocking the entrance, taking in the splendor of the lobby.

'Hasn't changed a bit,' Mother enthused, 'since the days of Gilbert and Sullivan! . . . Not that I was *around* back then, of course.'

'Good to know,' I said.

Actually, the lobby had changed quite a lot. During a lull back home at the shop, I'd read about the hotel's refurbishment in 2007, in which the lobby had expanded immensely, yet still retained the Art Deco and Edwardian styles for which London's most famous hotel was renowned.

'Remember what you promised?' I asked, taking her gently by the arm to clear the path for other guests coming in those revolving doors.

'I make many promises, dear, some that I actually keep, few that I keep track of. Enlighten me, ducky.'

'You promised, if I agreed to this trip, that you would *not* use your fake British accent.' Which she would often trot out to impress people, having of course quite the opposite effect.

Mother tossed her head. 'I would not characterize my accent as "fake." In the world of theater, I am quite well known for my amazing accents.'

If by that she meant, in the world of (Serenity, Iowa) theater, her accents had amazed many a theatergoer, keeping in mind one definition of 'amaze' is 'bewilder,' well . . . yes.

'I'm going to insist, Mother.'

'But I have various accents of the British variety – cockney, Yorkshire, Estuary English, and what of Irish and Scottish?'

'Not a one, Mother. Not a one.'

She unleashed the put-upon sigh of all put-upon sighs. 'Very well, if you're going to get your knickers in a twist.'

I followed her as she sashayed across the black-and-white checkered floor to the registration area, where two men, impeccably dressed in dark suits, were seated at a massive mahogany desk, in winged-back tapestry chairs, awaiting guests.

'Good morning, madam,' said one, addressing Mother. He was older than his co-worker, with a touch of gray at the temples. 'Checking in?'

'Ah surely am,' she drawled, in the manner of Blanche DuBois in her (unauthorized) musical version of *A Streetcar Named Desire* at the Serenity Playhouse. 'Mrs Viv-yun Boown, and Miss Bran-dah Boown.'

Well, she *had* kept her promise, technically.

'Welcome to the Savoy, ladies. Have you stayed with us before?'

'Ah suh-tin-lah haaave,' Mother said. Suddenly her Southern accent vanished, forgotten in a rush of memories. 'Back in the Swingin' Sixties! Carnaby Street, the Beatles, and free love . . . Those were the days, my friends! We thought they'd *never* end.'

The man's eyes rose to mine, as I had remained standing. I smiled back, then raised my eyebrows in quick succession. Welcome to the Savoy? Welcome to *my* world.

I patted Mother's shoulder. 'Seems to me you're doing fine here. Whistle if you need me.'

I wandered off to explore the rest of the lobby, which was divided into three seating areas, each like a living room of the rich and famous, separated by gilded columns to lend intimacy. Unlike the accommodations we more normally encountered, there were no nailed-to-the-wall oil paintings or glued-to-a-tabletop chintz vases.

But I admit I did feel shabby in my best clothes, a downstairs maid who snuck upstairs when the Lord and Lady were otherwise occupied.

The center rear of the lobby gave way to a descending flight of wide marble stairs that led to a landing with a few shops, and then on down to the fabled Thames Foyer, where I hoped we'd be having tea later. But for now I stayed put, up top.

Mother materialized beside me. 'Our room won't be ready until this afternoon,' she said. 'In the meantime, I'd like to take care of a bit of business.'

'What business is that?'

Our meeting at the new publisher wasn't scheduled till tomorrow morning.

'I promised Skylar James,' she said, 'that I'd drop by an antiques shop on Charing Cross Road.'

'Running errands in London? What's this about?'

She told me about the agreement with the necklace.

I snorted a laugh. 'Any other such shady dealings you haven't mentioned yet?'

'No, dear. And I'd hardly describe a favor for a fellow antiques dealer as "shady."'

The shady things that Mother didn't consider shady could fill a book. This one, for example.

'OK,' I said with a sigh, 'but we have limited time on this expensive little trip of ours. So after your errand, I want to do some touristy stuff.'

Leaving our bags behind – they would be delivered to our room in our absence – we took another of those classic black taxis, Mother giving the driver the address.

After we got in, she called, 'Tally ho!'

The cabbie chuckled, but I elbowed her. 'You promised!'

'That was an *unaccented* "tally ho," dear.'

She'd got me on another technicality!

We sat in silence on the brief ride to our destination, getting dropped off on Charing Cross near Old Compton Street, in an area I wouldn't call shabby, but not exactly upscale – more for locals than tourists.

The Old Curiosity Shop was sandwiched between a vaping store and a tiny Indian restaurant catering to mostly carry-out; a sign on the inside of the door's window indicated the shop was open.

An overhead bell announced us as we entered a claustrophobic world difficult to take in – one of taxidermy, medical items, the occult, and assorted oddities. As we made our way through a narrow aisle beneath a canopy of hanging, vaguely sinister puppets, a man suddenly appeared.

'How might I be of help?' he asked.

He was tall, cadaverous, with slicked-back silver hair, a long thin nose, and hollow cheeks, his mouth a mere slash. He reminded me of the older Peter Cushing, Dr Frankenstein in the old Hammer horror movies. But his eyes were friendly, even twinkling, giving me the sense that he enjoyed his slightly macabre surroundings.

'Vivian Borne,' Mother said – neither Southern belle nor cockney Brit. The atmosphere had smothered such pretensions, momentarily at least.

'Ah, yes,' he replied, the wrinkled face beaming, his teeth white and perfect and almost certainly courtesy of the National Health Service. 'Skylar James said you might pay a visit! Humphrey Westcott, at your disposal.' He offered a bony hand.

Mother took it, shook it, returned it, then without further preamble, announced, 'I'm afraid I have rather disappointing news for you, Mr Westcott.'

'Oh?' Shaggy eyebrows ascended a high forehead.

She touched the turquoise and silver jewelry at her throat. 'I have decided to keep the necklace.'

'I see.'

'I rather fell in love with it.'

That was *almost* an English accent – I narrowed one eye at her.

She went on, 'I've had so many compliments wearing it that I simply cannot bear to let it go.'

He nodded, expressionless. 'I see.'

'And the necklace *is* mine, after all – I paid for it and have a receipt.'

The shopkeeper leaned slightly forward for a better look at the necklace. Then admitted, 'It is a very nice example of Native American jewelry, especially for the price quoted me.' He straightened and gestured with a gracious open hand. 'And, yes, the turquoise stones indeed bring out your eyes.'

Rarely have I seen Mother blush, but that's just what she did.

'That's what *I've* been hearing!' she burbled. 'Everywhere I go. And turquoise isn't even in my color analysis!'

He gave her half a smile, his expression warm. 'I don't suppose you would consider finding a different necklace?'

'I really don't think I can locate one that I'd like better.'

One eyebrow went up. 'Even for a nice profit?'

Mother took a step back, as if affronted by the notion. 'I'm afraid not.'

Mr Westcott sighed. 'I can't deny my disappointment, Mrs Borne. But I do quite understand. When a woman falls in love with a piece of jewelry' – he tossed an ancient hand – 'there's no dissuading her.'

Mr Westcott seemed to speak from experience.

Her lips pressed together in a simpering smile. 'I knew you'd understand.'

The way I'd understood giving up my First Class seat.

'Well, Brandy,' Mother said, finally acknowledging my presence, 'as long as we're here, we should have a look around this fascinating establishment.'

'Please do,' the shopkeeper replied. 'Oh, and before you leave, perhaps you'd do *me* a favor.' He reached under the counter, brought out a hardcover book, its cover (depicting a train in a snowy landscape) protected by a plastic sleeve, and placed it on the counter.

'Skylar mentioned that his wife loves Agatha Christie. And I'd appreciate it if you'd give him this copy of *Murder on the Orient Express*. It's an inexpensive reprint, not worth much, at best a few pounds . . . but it will be my way of assuring Mr James there are no hard feelings regarding the necklace.'

'Of course,' Mother said graciously.

'I'll have it wrapped, and waiting.'

We began to browse the aptly named Old Curiosity Shop, because I was curious about why Mr Westcott thought much of anything here would ever sell. Perhaps he had a curious clientele.

He'd have to, because not just anybody wanted a mangy stuffed hedgehog, did they? Or a collection of bugs? A plaster dental mold of upper teeth? Or an old mannequin missing a glass eye?

I picked up a metal medieval-style letter opener, couldn't find a marking, and put it back down. What would I have done with it, in an e-mail age? Open junk mail?

After a polite amount of time, Mother and I returned to the counter, where the book lay wrapped in plain brown paper tied with twine.

Mr Westcott was not around. Since no little bell was available to ding, Mother called out. Once, then twice. But the shopkeeper seemed to have disappeared, like just another oddity in the shop. But then I heard his voice faintly coming from somewhere in the back, a one-sided conversation that told me he was on a phone.

Mother picked up the package, put it in her large tote bag, and we left, bell ringing behind us.

To avoid sounding like a travelogue, I will now give you the just highlights – or maybe it's low lights – of our afternoon of sightseeing. Imagine me with a slide show and a clicker.

At the Tower of London Mother proceeded to instruct a red-garbed Beefeater on the importance of introducing fruits and vegetables into his diet. As for me, I got reprimanded for taking pictures of the Crown Jewels, which I thought were replicas, never imagining the real things would be right out in the open like that.

At Madame Tussauds, Mother almost knocked over the figure of Madame herself, while I – sitting quietly on a bench – got mistaken for a waxwork by a small child, who screamed when I moved, and security descended.

In a line at the TKTS booth in Leicester Square we bought tickets for the next night's performance of *The Mousetrap* at the St. Martin's Theatre, and almost started a small riot when Mother was telling someone else in line about the Serenity Playhouse production of the venerable Agatha Christie mystery and revealed 'whodunit.'

'Doesn't *everyone* know by now?' Mother said, as we scurried away, tickets in hand.

Since it was nearing four, we caught a cab back to the

Savoy, where there wasn't time to freshen up in our room. So we proceeded to the Thames Foyer for high tea only to discover we needed reservations – something relatively unheard of in Serenity, Iowa. Fortunately, though, there had been a cancelation.

A woman in an elegant yet simple black dress escorted us into a large room, filtered with light via an elaborate glass dome. Below the dome stood a gazebo resembling a gigantic, gilded cage; instead of a bird, a black grand piano was encased therein, a tuxedo-sporting gentleman playing a Cole Porter tune.

We were seated in French Provincial chairs at a small round table, one of perhaps thirty surrounding the central gazebo. The atmosphere was elegant but relaxed, flowers on the tables adding the feeling of a garden party, linen-clothed tables set with china, sterling silver cutlery, and crystal.

Another woman in black brought us a silver three-tiered tray consisting of various finger sandwiches, scones, and pastries, plus our very own small silver tea set.

My stomach growled in a very un-refined manner.

'Well, isn't this delightful!' Mother said, using her hoity-toity (still technically non-UK) stage voice, attracting a pair of ladies near us. 'Quite comparable to the Majestic in Kuala Lumpur, and certainly better than the Sahn Eddar in Dubai.'

One woman whispered to the other, 'Is that someone?'

To which I turned and said, 'Absolutely not.'

Something had been gnawing at me besides my empty stomach.

Reaching for a scone, which was warm, I asked her, 'Did you notice anything odd when we were sightseeing?'

She had been taking a pretentiously delicate, pinkie-in-the-air sip of tea, and returned the cup to the saucer with equal over-precision. 'No. Why do you ask?'

I spread some clotted cream on the scone. 'I'm almost positive I spotted the same man at both the Tower and Tussauds, and also he walked by while we were getting those tickets. I think.'

Mother frowned. 'What did he look like?'

I shook my head. 'It's more the shirt he was wearing that

got my attention – a red-white-and-blue harlequin pattern with some kind of emblem.'

While she thoughtfully nibbled at a sandwich, I stuffed half the scone in my mouth. Hey, I was famished.

'Dear,' Mother finally said. 'Hundreds of people were at those same locales . . . and if someone was following us, wouldn't they choose a wardrobe that didn't make them stand out like that?'

'I guess so,' I said, and popped a sandwich in my mouth – cucumber with minty cream cheese. Yum. Bet you can't eat just one . . .

She went on, 'But if we *were* being followed, I wouldn't be a bit surprised.'

'Why?'

'Why *not*, after your buffoonery with the Crown Jewels.'

'*My* buffoonery? What about your buffoonery? Shall we talk about that? Recommending veggies to a Beefeater? Spoiling *The Mousetrap* for everybody after eighty years?'

'Please, dear, you're beginning to attract attention.'

And, after all, we were keeping a low profile.

I chomped hard on the end of an eclair, half wishing its contents would squirt out at her, then when it didn't, swallowed, said, 'We really should have bought something from that old gent. And by "we," I mean you.'

She shrugged. 'It's not my fault he disappeared before we could.'

'Well, we could go back to the shop. I think a sign said he was open until seven. There was a small Chinese puzzle box that wasn't too expensive, and would be a real conversation piece in our store.'

'I did see that myself. Jolly good idea.'

'Moth-*er* . . .'

A tray of cakes was served, and we stayed until the end of tea, when Mother was presented with a bill for one-hundred-and-fifty-two pounds. So suddenly I didn't feel guilty about consuming nearly everything in sight but the linen tablecloth.

Outside, we hailed another cab. The sunny afternoon had disappeared, replaced with gray clouds and a light drizzle, promising inclement weather to come. But this was London, after all. You kind of wanted it to rain, and hoped a fog would roll in.

Back at the shop, we found that the sign on the inside of the door's window had been turned to CLOSED.

'But it's not seven yet,' I lamented.

Mother, never one to be deterred by a closed sign, tried the knob, and to our surprise, the door opened, the bell announcing guests.

But no Mr Westcott came forward to greet us.

'There must be an office in the rear, dear,' Mother said. 'You look while I'll retrieve the puzzle box.'

I wound my way through a labyrinth of passageways, lined with bizarre framed paintings and prints, and ending at a door that was partially ajar.

'Mr Westcott?' I called out. 'It's Brandy Borne. We've come back to buy something. Mr Westcott?'

I pushed the door open. Seated behind a small desk, leaning back in his office chair, was the shopkeeper, staring with wide but unseeing eyes, mouth open but silent, the medieval-style letter opener protruding from his chest.

I bolted for a nearby wastebasket, and said goodbye to the expensive Thames Foyer high-tea cuisine.

A Trash 'n' Treasures Tip

Dealers who buy foreign antiques often find the items don't resonate with buyers back home. So keep your investment low, in case you're stuck with that silver abacus teething ring.

FOUR
Carry On Constable

As I knelt over the wastebasket, a tissue floated in front of me like a small, stray ghost. I took it from Mother's hand.

'Isn't that a shame,' she said with what seemed genuine sympathy. 'All those exquisite sandwiches and pastries, consigned to a circular file!'

I straightened and wiped my mouth with the tissue. 'Definitely not as sweet coming up as going down . . . You *do* note the dead man in the chair?'

'Certainly, dear. Nothing wrong with *my* eyes.'

Except the onset of glaucoma and cataracts.

She was saying, 'I had a *feeling* all was not kosher, what with the closed sign, and the door unlocked.'

'No food references, Mother, please. So, suspecting foul play afoot, you sent *me* for a look?'

Her eyebrows rose. 'Well, in my defense, dear, I didn't think the poor man would necessarily be dead – perhaps just ye olde bonk on the head.'

Steady on my feet again, I glanced around, then it came to me, and I gestured rather frantically. 'Mother, my *fingerprints* are on that letter opener!'

'There are any number of letter openers offered for sale in this peculiar establishment. What particular letter opener?'

'The particular one stuck in the dead man's chest!'

'Yo ho ho and a bottle of rum,' Mother said cheerfully, as she leaned toward the body for a closer look with those eyes that had nothing wrong with them. 'Is *that* what that is? A letter opener?'

'Yes! Yes! I picked it up earlier.'

Mother's eyes grew even larger behind the lenses. 'Oh, my. Then I would have to say you may well be in a pickle.'

'You mean *we're* in a pickle.'

A one-shouldered shrug. 'Not meaning to pass the buck, dear, but *my* prints aren't on the murder weapon.'

So she was throwing me under the double-decker bus.

I raised my chin. 'True. Still, you're sure to be seen as an accomplice.'

Mother thought about that. 'A definite possibility.'

'So, what are *we* going to do?' I asked. 'My vote is call the police.'

'The constabulary, dear.'

'Whatever! Bobbies on bicycles two by two, for all I care.'

She raised a forefinger. 'Calm yourself. Losing control of the situation is no way to react.'

'How do we control finding a murder victim with my prints on the weapon?'

Eyebrows up again. 'Wipe your prints off the handle, mayhap? Take our quiet leave?'

I frowned at her. 'Absolutely not. How can you even suggest that?'

'A weak moment. It isn't like me to just scurry away from a murder scene. Obviously, before we ring the authorities, we should search this place – it's our only hope of clearing ourselves.'

'Search the place! For *what*?'

'Clues, dear! Clues! *Something* got poor Mr Westcott killed, beyond his questionable taste in antiques.'

I suppose I should have used better sense than to go along with her, but I wasn't anxious to be grilled ever so politely by the London police. Maybe we'd turn something up that demonstrated my innocence.

'All right,' I heard myself saying. 'But you look in here – even empty, my stomach couldn't take it.'

While Mother remained with the deceased proprietor, I returned to the outer shop.

I slipped behind the glass counter to the cash register and, again with a sleeve-wrapped finger, rang up a sale for the cash drawer to open. Money was within, indicating this hadn't been a robbery. My sleeve-wrapped finger shut it.

Then I circled the counter to peer at the contents under glass, which was mostly antique jewelry, coins, silver trinkets, and military medals. Everything appeared undisturbed, with no empty spaces between.

I wandered the aisles trying to recall quick snapshots my mind had taken of the dozens upon dozens of items on display – but how would I really know if something was missing? Nothing left to do but get back behind the counter to wait for Mother.

Suddenly, a shadowy figure appeared outside the window trying to look in, and I ducked down.

And waited.

After a minute, Mother crawled over to me.

'Are we down here for a reason?' she whispered.

'No. Just thought it would be a bit of bloody fun.'

'Very droll, dear.'

I nodded toward the front window. 'Someone was outside.'

'Well, they're gone now,' she said. 'Help me up, dear. The spirit is willing but the knees are weak.'

I helped her to her feet. 'Well?'

'Our late host still had his wallet in a pocket, plus a cell phone and some keys.'

My eyes opened wide. 'You *searched* him?'

'Of course.'

I shivered. 'Ooooough.'

'No room for the squeamish at a crime scene, dear. Buck up! Did you find anything?'

'Cash still in the register.'

She nodded. 'That, and the wallet, along with credit cards, says this wasn't about money.'

We fell silent for a moment.

I said, 'Maybe you were right, before.'

'No question about that.' She frowned. 'In what respect?'

'Maybe we *should* wipe the handle of the letter opener.'

Mother was withdrawing her phone from her bag. 'I'm afraid that might only make matters worse.'

'Worse than me getting charged with murder?'

'Smudged prints, a wiped-off handle, and us at the scene?

Ill-advised.' She punched in 999, the UK 911, then spoke, succinctly. 'Hello . . . I'd like to report the discovery of a dead body.'

We went outside to wait. On the sidewalk (or pavement, as they called it here) we stood quietly as pedestrians passed and cars glided by in a cool overcast accompanied by sprinkles that were as close to London rain or fog as we seemed likely to get. Within a few minutes, a siren could be heard, announcing the arrival of a yellow-and-blue checkered four-door BMW with flashing blue lights.

A milk-chocolate-skinned female exited the driver's side; she was attired in a long-sleeved white shirt, black-and-white checked cravat, black slacks and shoes, and the traditional black hat with center badge and checkered band.

'Did you ring about a body?' she asked, her accent Indian, name tag reading CONSTABLE BANERJEE.

'Yes, I did,' Mother said, stepping forward. 'The shop owner is in the back room. No need to call the paramedics, I assure you. The man is quite dead.'

She'd said this casually, as if reporting London's current weather conditions.

The constable frowned. 'You're quite certain of that?'

'Well, stabbed in the chest as he is, he's certainly not resting.'

I had a terrible moment where I thought she might go into the Monty Python 'Dead Parrot' sketch, since British comedy was one of the few things that could make her laugh.

'And your names?' the constable inquired politely.

'Vivian Borne,' Mother said, then gestured to me. 'My daughter Brandy. We're in London for a few days from the States to see our publisher, and decided to visit this antiques store, where we made this unfortunate discovery.'

'I'm terribly sorry,' Constable Banerjee said, 'but I will have to detain you both. I'll need statements taken at the station. Will you please wait here?'

'Certainly,' Mother replied. 'We want to do whatever we can to be of help.'

Within a minute, the officer returned, almost simultaneous

with the arrival of a police van. Two male officers clambered out, and hurried into the building.

Mother turned to Constable Banerjee. 'There is just one little bitty, itsy bitsy, teensy-weensy thing we might mention.'

'Yes?'

'You may find my daughter's fingerprints on the letter-opener handle.'

I glared at Mother. 'You couldn't even wait until we got to the station?'

Until then, the constable had been polite, even sympathetic toward her American cousins who'd had their nice trip to London spoiled by the ugliness of death.

Now she slapped handcuffs on me, barked for us to get into the back of her car, and we were driven off, the vehicle's siren screaming and blue lights flashing. Very soon we were going through a steel-door security entrance and into the center courtyard of a large cream-colored stone building that took up the entire block.

Constable Banerjee hauled us out of the vehicle and took us inside, where Mother and I were divested of our belongings, fingerprinted, photographed, swabbed for DNA, and – as Mother kept shouting, 'I demand to see the American ambassador' – unceremoniously deposited in adjoining holding cells.

Resignedly, I made myself as comfortable as one could on a hard bench with a thin blue plastic mat, and waited for whatever came next.

(*Note to reader*: Mother *insisted* that our separate interrogations be transcribed for realism, and presented as a two-act play. I know, I know . . . I tried.)

WITNESS FOR THE PERSECUTION
a play by Vivian Borne

Place: Charing Cross Police Station, London.
Time: Mid-April.
Setting: a small interview room with one table and two chairs (across from each other), and a two-way mirror. On

the table is a recording/intercom
device, and box of tissues.
Characters: Agent Hasty (fifty-ish),
Vivian Borne (an attractive woman of a
certain age), Brandy Borne (early thirties), and a policewoman, 'Lackey,' a
minor part ideal for an inexperienced
ingenue, or investor.

ACT ONE

Hasty
(*activating the recorder*)
Interview with Vivian Borne at Charing
Cross Station on fifteen April of the
present year, time nineteen thirty-six,
conducted by Agent Hasty. (*Pause*) Have
you been cautioned, Mrs Borne?

Vivian
Often . . . not that it ever seems to
help.

(*hold for audience laughter*)

Hasty
(*ignoring remark*)
You do not have to say anything. But it
may harm your defense if you do not
mention when questioned something which
you later rely on in court. Anything you
do say may be given in evidence. What is
your name?

Vivian
You've already said it, dear.

>   Hasty
Your *full* name . . . address and date of
birth.

>   Vivian
Vivian Jensen Borne, twenty-six hundred
Mulberry Avenue, Serenity, Iowa, USA.
As to my date of birth, that, sir, is
none of your business.

>   Hasty
It *is* my business. Please answer.

>   Vivian
Then I plead the Fifth.

>   Hasty
The Fifth Amendment to the Constitution
of the United States of America does not
apply in the UK.

>   Vivian
Then why did you caution me?

(*pause for smattering of applause*)

>   Hasty
In what circumstances would revealing
your age incriminate you?

>   Vivian
Because I've been lying about it for
years.

(*hold for audience laughter*)

>   Hasty
>   (*not amused*)
We'll let that go for now.

                        Vivian
                       (*archly*)
Am I allowed a barrister?

                        Hasty
If you know a solicitor in London, we
will contact him or her. Otherwise, one
can be provided, if you don't mind
sitting in your cell a while.

                        Vivian
Define 'a while.'

                        Hasty
                       (*shrugs*)
Twenty-four to thirty-six hours. Our
duty solicitors are kept quite busy.

                        Vivian
Well, it's a big bad city, so I'm not
surprised. And the requisite phone
call?

                        Hasty
After the interview.

                        Vivian
Very well. I waive my right to legal
representation during this interview.
(*cocks her head*) *Agent* Hasty, not
'Inspector' . . . isn't that MI5? I just
loved that show *Spooks*, which, by the
way, was called *MI5* in the States,
perhaps to keep it from being mistaken
for a Stephen King story. (*a beat*) But I
do have one complaint about series ten
— and it's a biggie! They should have
let Harry and Ruth go off happily
together into the sunset, instead of

killing her off. Oops! Delayed spoiler
alert! (*another beat*) Anyway, why would
MI5 be interested in this particular
murder?

                    Hasty
            (*consulting a paper*)
You made a comment to Constable Banerjee
that I'd like to confirm for the record.
You stated that your daughter's fingerprints are on the murder weapon . . . is
that correct?

                    Vivian
I said it was likely that would be. That
is, Brandy told me she'd picked up
the letter opener when we'd been there
earlier today. I didn't actually see
her do it.

                    Hasty
Then you'd gone to the shop earlier?

                    Vivian
That's right, late this morning. As an
antiques dealer myself, I'd heard about
the Old Curiosity Shop and thought we
might find it interesting.

                    Hasty
        (*suspecting there's more to it*)
Ah-huh. So why return hours later?

                    Vivian
            (*shifting in chair*)
Well . . . after we did some sightseeing, and had tea at the Savoy, I felt
rather bad about not buying anything
from Mr Westcott, and insisted that we

go back and get something. That's when I
discovered the poor man.

                    Hasty
How much time passed between finding the
body, and when you called the emergency
number?

                    Vivian
               (*stalling*)
I'm feeling a little peaked. Might I
please have some tea - with cream and
sugar - and perhaps a biscuit? Or two?

                    Hasty
        (*presses the intercom button*)
Some tea for Mrs Borne.

                    Vivian
            (*saccharine sweet*)
How hospitable.

                    Hasty
The question?

                    Vivian
Hit the 'refresh' button, would you,
dear?

(*hold for audience laughter*)

                    Hasty
            (*losing patience*)
I asked you, how much time passed
between finding the body, and when you
called the emergency number?

                    Vivian
                (*rubbing her chin*)
Well, let me see - I was in quite a
state of shock, as you can well imagine,
so it's hard to pinpoint exactly . . .

*Lackey knocks on door, enters room,
places styrofoam cup in front of Vivian.*

                    Vivian
Thank you, dear.

                    Lackey
You're welcome.

                    Vivian
                  (*to her*)
And thank you for saying 'You're
welcome.' Back in the States all we seem
to hear these days is 'no problem' or
'no worries,' which are all negative
words. Plus those responses make it
sound as though you're doing someone a
favor, rather than attending to your
job.

                    Hasty
              (*gruffly to Lackey*)
That will be all.

Lackey leaves.

                    Vivian
            (*takes a sip from cup*)
How delightful! Earl Grey, is it? My
personal preference is PG Tips with its
malty flavor and robust taste . . . the

perfect piquant pick-me-up for after
dinner.

                    Hasty
                 (*irritated*)
The *question*, Mrs Borne. Surely you've
had enough time to come up with an
answer. Otherwise, we can always check
the CCTV for the time you entered the
shop, and when the call was received by
the dispatcher.

                    Vivian
No, no, I don't think that will be
necessary. Ol' Big Brother does keep
watch in the UK, doesn't he? . . . I'd
say somewhere between five and twenty-
five minutes. Give or take a few minutes.

                    Hasty
And that's as close as you can
estimate?

                    Vivian
I'm afraid so.

                    Hasty
Did you touch the body?

                    Vivian
Yes. To check for a pulse.

                    Hasty
           (*nasty, knowing little smile*)
Did you take any photographs of the body
with your cell phone? Or rifle through
any desk drawers?

                    Vivian
                    (*shocked*)
Agent Hasty! I'm afraid someone has
been telling tales out of school!

                    Hasty
Let's just say your reputation casts a
long shadow.

                    Vivian
                    (*indignant*)
Clear across the *pond*? . . . I wouldn't
believe any of what you've heard,
especially if it comes from Police Chief
Tony Cassato. And regarding touching
anything or taking photos, as a retired
sheriff I *certainly* know not to disturb a
crime scene.

                    Hasty
That still doesn't answer the question.

                    Vivian
                    (*one-shoulder shrug*)
Granted, I *may* have *inadvertently*
touched a few things, while in a state of
shock. (*a beat*) Was there a security
camera in the office?

                    Hasty
Unfortunately, no.

                    Vivian
                    (*disingenuous*)
Oh, that *is* unfortunate. It would
certainly tell you a lot, and of course
refresh my memory.

                    Hasty
             (*a hard stare*)
Wouldn't it, though.

                    Vivian
             (*cheerfully*)
If there's nothing more, I'd like to
make that phone call. I should notify
our editor at the publishing house as
to our whereabouts.

                    Hasty
     (*finger on recorder stop button*)
End of interview with Vivian Borne,
time, twenty thirteen.

INTERMISSION

(*backstage pep-talk*)

Mother: The second act is plagued by dull
stretches, dear. Do try to pep it up!

Brandy: Sorry — I'm a little too bummed
out about possibly being charged with
murder to be peppy.

Mother: I'm not asking you to be Neil
Simon! Embellish! It's a playwright's
prerogative. Otherwise the audience
will be leaving the theater in droves!

ACT II

Setting: same.
Time: fifteen minutes later.
At rise: Hasty, looking a little beleaguered from his interview with Vivian,
is seated across the table from Brandy.

                    Hasty
          (*activating the recorder*)
Interview with Brandy Borne at Charing
Cross Station on April the fifteenth of
the present year, time, twenty twenty-
eight, conducted by Agent Hasty. (*Pause*)
Have you been informed of your rights, Ms
Borne?

                    Brandy
Yes. By Constable Banerjee as I was
handcuffed.

                    Hasty
                 (*politely*)
Would you like some tea?

                    Brandy
Or coffee if you have some. Black.

                    Hasty
             (*into intercom*)
One coffee, please. Black. (*to Brandy*)
For the record, please state your full
name, address, and date of birth.

                    Brandy
Brandy Jensen Borne, twenty-six-hundred
Mulberry Avenue, Serenity, Iowa, United
States. Born June eighteenth, nineteen
hundred and (Vivian: Dear! A woman never
tells!).

                    Hasty
Why did you and your mother go to the
Old Curiosity Shop?

                    Brandy
She was supposed to sell a necklace for

a fellow dealer back home, to avoid any
duty fees or whatever taxes there might
be. (*a beat*) But Mother had decided to
keep the necklace, so we went there so
she could tell Mr Westcott personally.

                    Hasty
What was the name of the dealer back
home?

                    Brandy
Skylar James. He owns a store in
Serenity — The Trading Post.

*Lackay knocks on door, opens it, enters,
hands Brandy the coffee.*

                    Brandy
Thank you.

                    Lackey
       (*unhappy with her role, here and in
                    life*)
No problem. No worries. (*leaves room*)

(*hold for laughs*)

                    Hasty
Was Mr Westcott upset that he didn't get
the necklace?

                    Brandy
       (*sips coffee, considering*)
Maybe a little - but certainly not
enough to make a scene. He seemed to
understand Mother had fallen in love
with the item. In fact, he gave Mother a
book to take back to Skylar to show that
he had no hard feelings.

Hasty
The book in her tote bag?

Brandy
(*a jolt*)
Oh . . . I suppose you did go through our
things. Yes, that one. (*a beat*) It's not
valuable. We have the same edition back
home, in better condition actually.

Hasty
Now, later, when you returned to the
premises and your mother discovered
the body—

Brandy
(*interrupting*)
I found Mr Westcott in the office. She
sent me off to look for him when he wasn't
at the front of the shop. (*a beat*) Oh! I
forgot to mention — I threw up in the
wastebasket by the desk. (*sarcastic-
ally*) Just in case I (*air quotes*) 'might
need to rely upon it in court.'

Hasty
(*small smile, liking her spunk*)
What did your mother do after you told
her you'd found the body?

Brandy
She joined me in Mr Westcott's office. I
told her I recognized the handle of the
letter opener because I'd picked it up
this morning.

Hasty
And what did she say?

                      Brandy
That we should look around for a motive
before calling the police, because —
since I would be implicated — we needed
to find any clues that might help me.

                      Hasty
Was the intention to tamper with the
scene of the crime?

                      Brandy
Of course not! Merely to point out
anything helpful to the reporting
officers.

                      Hasty
And what exactly did you both do?

                      Brandy
Mother looked around the office where -
according to her - she found Mr
Westcott's wallet, his cell phone, and
some keys in his pockets. The wallet had
money and credit cards, so this obviously was not a robbery. Meanwhile, out
front, I checked the cash register,
which also had cash.

                      Hasty
Anything else?

                      Brandy
I can't speak for her - except that she
probably took photos of the crime scene
on her phone. But I did look around to
see if any merchandise was obviously
missing.

                    Hasty
And?

                    Brandy
                  (*shrugs*)
Who could tell with all that stuff.

                    Hasty
What made you think your behavior was
appropriate?

                    Brandy
Did I say I did? On the other hand, we
have written a number of published true-
crime books, and Mother *is* a former
sheriff. We have some experience with
murder cases, although I wish we didn't.

                    Hasty
                 (*muttering*)
As do I.

                    Brandy
Am I going to be charged with murder? I
didn't kill Mr Westcott. How could I? He
was alive when we left him this morning
. . . and I'm sure you can find us on
various security cameras, sightseeing.

                    Hasty
                  (*wryly*)
You did make quite an impression at the
Tower, and museum.

                    Brandy
             (*lightbulb moment*)
You had someone following us! The guy in
the rugby shirt!

                    Hasty
               (*mildly surprised*)
You noticed him?

                    Brandy
Duh! Next time don't have him wear
anything that gaudy.

                    Hasty
                  (*shrugs*)
We've been trying to get away from tell-
tale suit-and-tie.

                    Brandy
                (*helpfully*)
Maybe try something in between circus
and office?

                    Hasty
                (*moving on*)
And, no, you're not going to be charged
with murder. Westcott was killed in the
mid-afternoon.

                    Brandy
Well, that's a relief! I mean, that I'm
not going to be charged, not that Mr
Westcott was killed.

(*hold for possible audience titters*)

                    Hasty
              (*turning serious*)
However, you and Mrs Borne could easily
be charged with interfering at a crime
scene. (*suspenseful pause*) But . . . I
think the best solution is to put you
both on the first plane back to the
States in the morning. Until that can

be arranged, you'll remain in your
cells.

                    Brandy
                  (*outraged*)
What?! You mean we can't spend the night
at the Savoy? We've already paid for the
room!

                    Hasty
Murder can be a nuisance.

                    Brandy
                  (*indignant*)
I want to make a call to Chief Tony
Cassato in Serenity.

                    Hasty
Very well . . . but I'm afraid it won't
help you.

                    Brandy
And why is that?

                    Hasty
                  (*little smile*)
It was at Chief Cassato's suggestion
that we're keeping you here overnight.
(*into recorder*) End of interview with
Brandy Borne, time, twenty-one twelve.

                  CURTAIN

(*applause*)

(*curtain call — repeat as needed*)

OK, curtain down, and Brandy back.
   If you're wondering, I didn't contact Tony with my one

phone call (I didn't call anybody), because I knew I'd lose my temper. Nor did I tell Mother, until much later, that my fiancé was responsible for our very special overnight stay.

Not that it mattered to her, as she seemed to feel at home in her cell, regaling a female officer – delivering a late supper – with jailhouse tales from back home. Even through the thick wall I could hear Mother's theatrical voice.

'I've even been charged with felony murder,' Mother was saying. 'It was a miscarriage of justice, of course, but I was in for about a week until cleared. And during that time I became top dog, like in *Wentworth* on the telly, organized a female theater group among the prisoners, and still managed to obtain a clue vital to the murder for which I'd been charged. I was having so much fun, I didn't want to leave.'

'Well, Mrs Borne, I'll be back to collect the tray . . .'

'After I was sprung,' Mother pressed on, 'I was able to talk prison officials into letting the group perform for other inmates. We were doing the Midwest circuit – Des Moines, Galesburg, Omaha, and Kansas City, until two of our actors escaped during a performance. How sad! We were on our way to the bigtime, like San Quentin, Sing Sing, and Folsom – such a shame Alcatraz had closed – but that brought the curtain down abruptly on my prison theater group.'

I barely could hear the constable's words: 'What was the play?'

'*The Vagina Monologues.*'

Shortly, the lock on my steel door clicked open, and the officer entered with my tray – a blonde wearing the typical guard attire, her hair in a chignon, sans hat.

Seated on the bench, I said, 'You had to ask, didn't you?'

A small smile, but otherwise the woman remained professional, handing me a plastic tray of food. 'It's not the Savoy, but will have to do.'

I balanced the tray on my knees. 'Thank you. Sausage and spuds, huh?'

'No, bangers and mash. I'll bring you another blanket, and a few necessaries including a toothbrush and paste, when I return.'

I nodded. 'Do you know when we'll be leaving in the morning? I'd hate to oversleep.'

Another smile. 'It's being sorted.'

She left, the door clicking behind her.

The following morning – I actually slept like a rock, if a rock can have bad, girls-in-prison-movie dreams – I freshened up as best I could and had a breakfast of toast and eggs and coffee, which I barely had time to scarf down before being informed we were about to leave for the airport.

We were processed out, given back our possessions, and this time, escorted out the front door; a police van was waiting with our luggage, collected from the Savoy and stowed in the wayback.

As Mother and I were about to climb in behind the grille, a young woman in business attire, tentatively approached.

'Vivian? Brandy? I'm Olivia Adams.'

Good Lord! Our editor!

The police escort was urging us into the vehicle.

Mother, looking as delighted as if she'd found an old farthing on the sidewalk, said, 'How wonderful to meet you! So sorry we can't make our get-together today, but it seems we're being run out of town on a rail – er, *tail* . . . of a Boeing 747!' Then, in a Groucho Marx impression, she sang, 'Hello, I must be going!'

And so go we did, leaving behind a very confused-looking and possibly appalled editor.

In the van, I turned to Mother. 'Boeing 747?'

'Just a little joke, dear. You're always claiming that I have no sense of humor, when clearly—'

'No! I mean, we're not going home on an Airbus?'

'I'm afraid not, dear,' she replied. 'After the fee of re-booking our tickets, we couldn't afford the 380. And only one First Class seat on the 747.'

'What, am I going to sit on your lap?'

'Of course not. You'll be in coach.'

With no applause or food upgrade.
The perfect ending to a perfectly terrible trip.
Pip pip.

A Trash 'n' Treasures Tip

Buying foreign coins can be a lucrative way to invest your
money, but only if you understand the business. Just because
a coin is old, doesn't make it valuable. Sometimes a farthing
is only worth . . . a farthing.

FIVE
Carry On Cowboy

I was still in bed at noon when Mother entered my Art Decorated domain and roused me.

'Tony's dropped by,' she said excitedly.

Jet-lagged after the long flight home – in coach! – I pulled myself up, propped against the pillows, and growled, 'I'm not speaking to that louse.'

Mother, dressed for the day, sat at the foot of the bird's-eye maple bed. 'Don't you think that's a little short-sighted, dear? You should hear what the louse has to say for himself.'

Yes, I had told her Tony was responsible for our incarceration, and she probably suspected there would be fireworks between us – or at least, a sparkler or two – and, with her theatrical bent, she wouldn't want to miss it.

She was saying, 'I know *I* want to hear what he has to say. I spent a night in the nick because of him!'

I grunted. 'You'd rather spend a night in jail than a week at Disneyland.'

'Wouldn't anyone over ten? Anyway, he's brought dear little Sushi back.'

'Oh, *fine*,' I said childishly, and threw back the covers. 'I'll come down. But *don't* tell him! Make him wait.'

I was doubly irritated because Sushi hadn't dashed up to see me.

After Mother left, I staggered over to the 1930s round-mirrored dressing table that matched the bed, dresser, and nightstand, and sat on the button-tufted stool.

I looked dreadful. No, make that 'scary.' Hair a mess, mascara smeared, face puffy, plaid pajamas tattered because I'd rather spend money on clothes people could see. Victoria's Secret was a well-kept one in my bedroom.

Still, I made no adjustments to my appearance – Tony might

as well get used to me first thing in the morning – as I put on a Minnie Mouse bathrobe and a pair of moose slippers that my BFF had given me as a joke, which were warmer and more comfy than my favorite Uggs.

My fiancé was standing in the midst of our Victorian-appointed living room, holding Sushi in his arms like a hairy baby. He turned toward me expressionless as I descended the stairs.

As I walked toward him, the moose slippers' plastic eyes with beads swirled Looney Tunes-like in opposite directions.

Mother appeared to have made herself scarce, but don't you believe it – she'd be lurking close by, hand cupped to one ear.

'I'm not speaking to you,' I announced to him petulantly.

Sushi, upon hearing the inflection of my voice, jumped out of Tony's arms, and trotted loyally over to me.

'I understand,' Tony said.

'And I may not speak to you for a long time.'

Tony nodded. 'That's your prerogative. You, uh . . . mean starting now? Because you have said several things already.'

He had just the tiniest, barely discernible smile going, and that – and his complacency – infuriated me.

I lashed out: 'How could you do that to us? Mother, maybe . . . but to *me*? Why couldn't we have stayed one more day at the Savoy? And it was *embarrassing*, running into our new editor outside the police station! We'll probably lose our *contract* over this!'

'So, then, you like writing those books with your mother.'

'No! I hate it! Not the writing, but what we have to go through to get the raw material. You think I *like* crime scenes?'

'You do turn up there frequently.' Tony spread his hands, placatingly. He banished all hint of a smile. 'Look, I'll explain everything if you and Vivian will just sit down with me at the dining-room table for a few minutes.'

The chief had long ago learned he was at a disadvantage in the living room, finding it difficult to discuss anything while perched on a small Queen Anne chair that nowadays fit only a child.

'Was I summoned?' Mother called out from the kitchen.

'Yes,' I called back. 'Olly, olly, oxen free!'

Soon we were gathered around our Duncan Phyfe table, she and I across from each other, Tony standing at the head, as if he were about to carve up a turkey. Or two.

He began, 'I'm sorry you spent the night in a cell, and that your trip was cut short. I didn't take that step lightly.'

I said, 'You admit you arranged it.'

'Yes. But I felt all of that was necessary. You had compromised an ongoing official investigation at that antiques shop you visited.'

This was news to me, but not Mother, who clarified, 'An investigation conducted by MI5.'

He nodded.

I goggled at her. 'How could you know that?'

She shrugged. 'Because we were interviewed by an *agent*, dear, not an inspector.'

'Oh.' I hadn't paid any attention to Hasty's title, too distracted by my perilous position to absorb such petty details.

Mother, her focus back on Tony, said archly, 'Be that as it may, Chief Cassato, I see no valid reason why we should have been jugged overnight, and then given the unceremonious boot out of Britain.'

'Not even,' Tony asked, 'if your lives were in danger?'

Now Mother was doing the goggling, her eyes bulging behind her large lenses like a rubber squeeze doll's. 'Really and truly in *danger*?' she asked, more excited than alarmed.

'That was the implication,' Tony replied.

She swung toward me. '*Now* we have a book for our new publisher!'

I ignored that, asking him, 'In danger because we found Mr Westcott's body?'

His eyes hardened. 'That might have been enough. Or perhaps the possibility of you and Vivian having seen something – and yes, I know you searched the shop.'

I raised my chin. 'Not searched. Looked around, not disturbing anything. Ascertaining that Mr Westcott hadn't been killed for money was the extent of it.' I looked at Mother. 'Isn't that right?'

She didn't answer me, instead swiveled toward Tony to ask bluntly, 'What *aren't* you telling us, Chief?'

He met her gaze coolly. 'I hardly think MI5 is going to take a small-town police chief into its confidence.'

Mother pressed. 'Is there some connection between Westcott and Skylar James? You're aware of our reason for going to the Old Curiosity Shop?'

'I am. And according to Agent Hasty, the transaction with the necklace – or lack thereof – had nothing to do with their surveillance.'

Mother looked unconvinced. 'Then, no Serenity connection, no London connection?'

'Or French, for that matter – no. And I don't know whether this Westcott character was the object of the investigation or just collateral damage.'

Really, Tony had bailed us out by getting us locked in. We'd been in way over our heads.

Mother didn't seem to take it that way, though, huffing, 'If we hadn't been sent packing, *I* could have found out.'

'You'd have tried to,' Tony said flatly.

And could have gotten us killed, I thought with a shiver.

Tony leaned forward, hands flat on the table, giving his next words more weight. 'And I have a message from Agent Hasty . . . any further meddling on your part will bring charges. And don't look to *me* to help you fight extradition.'

Mother shrugged. 'I don't see how I could "meddle" from afar.'

As if distance was any deterrent to her.

I said, 'Tony, we owe you an apology. What you did was for the best. Right, Mother? *Mother?*'

'I'll grant your well-meaning intentions,' she told him, grudgingly. 'Anyway, the experience in the clink will give me the opportunity to write Charing Cross Police Station about the deplorable conditions of their holding cells. I ask you, would a fresh coat of paint break the Bank of England? How about a peaceful mural of a tropical paradise to bring a bit of cheer to its wayward residents?'

Getting up, I smirked at Tony. 'I'll see you to the door.'

We left Mother at the table, pondering other decorative jailhouse touches, her voice trailing off, 'A reading table in the commons area, with some magazines and paperbacks, would help pass the time . . .'

In the entryway, I faced Tony, feeling small next to his formidable frame.

'You don't have to worry about her,' I told him. 'She's already onto something else. A local prospect for that new book.'

'Dare I ask?'

'Ruth Hassler.'

Tony's brow furrowed. 'The woman who had the fatal fall down her stairs a few months ago?'

I nodded. 'Anything to it?'

He shook his head. 'An accident.'

'Good. Mother will be spinning her wheels.'

'What about the new book?'

'I'm trying to move her into fictional murders. Less chance of "collateral damage" . . . particularly of us being it.'

'Good to hear.' He touched the tip of my nose with a fore-finger. 'We OK?'

I smiled. 'Yes. But prescribing a lasagna dinner at your cabin this weekend would alleviate any concerns you might have about my well-being, doctor.'

'Deal.'

After Tony left, I returned to the dining room to consult Mother about breakfast, but she wasn't there . . . nor was she in the kitchen.

I found her in the library at the overstuffed bookshelves, on a step stool, searching the titles.

'What are you looking for?' I asked.

Instead of answering, Mother exclaimed, '*Ah!* There it is.'

She plucked out a book, stepped down, and came over to show me: a vintage reprint of *Murder on the Orient Express* by the great Agatha Christie.

I said, 'That looks like the book Westcott gave you.'

'It is, dear, or that is, another copy thereof. Same publisher, same edition, even the identical cover of a train in snowy landscape, protected in a plastic sleeve.'

I waggled a finger. 'You're going to switch books so you can have a better copy!'

Mother splayed a hand on her chest. 'Brandy, you cut me to the quick! How could you even *think* such a thing!'

'It was easy,' I said, quoting another great mystery writer.

She looked toward the heavens – or the ceiling. 'How sharper than a serpent's tooth it is to have a thankless child.'

'"Me thinks the lady doth protest too much."'

Mother drew me over to the library table, where Westcott's copy of the same book rested on top of its brown paper wrapping.

'The only thing I had to read on the flight,' she said, gesturing to the volume, 'was this book in my carry on. And unfortunately, as I proceeded, many of the corners of the pages simply crumbled due to the aged condition of its cheap paper.'

I picked up the novel and thumbed through it, more shards flaking off.

'See what you mean,' I said.

'We'll give him *my* nice edition – isn't that generous of me?'

I frowned skeptically. 'How much do you have into that copy?'

'Two dollars. But the protective Mylar cover alone is worth seventy cents.'

The soul of generosity, Vivian Borne.

'OK,' I said. 'I'll add Westcott's book to Dumpster Dan's box in our trunk, and drop it off at the recycle center sometime.' Mother had already gone through the box and salvaged a couple of Stout and Christie reprints.

She had stopped listening, if she'd ever had been. Heading toward the kitchen, Mother announced, 'We'll take my copy to Skylar after breakfast.'

'You mean, *you'll* take it to him,' I said, tagging after, Sushi doing the same with me. 'I plan on relieving Joe at the shop.'

Mother was shaking her head. 'It's started to rain so I can't take the Vespa. You'll have to drive me . . . plus I have a few more places I need to go.'

'Hey, I'm not your deputy-cum-chauffeur anymore!'

'Of course you are. Ex officio, as am I. Still a badge in my purse, remember!'

We were in the kitchen now.

'Then I want a big breakfast,' I groused. 'Omelet, American fries, toast, bacon *and* sausage.' I can always be bought off by way of my stomach.

Only later, tooling downtown, Mother riding shotgun, Sushi left behind, I didn't feel so good after consuming all that food.

I found an empty spot in front of The Trading Post and pulled in.

Mother – with the swapped, re-wrapped book in her tote on her lap – said, 'Let me do the talking.'

'I have no intention of saying anything.'

'Good.'

'Fine.'

It was going to be a long day.

And a wet one. We exited the Fusion, then made a dash for the door, the rain pelting us momentarily, the sky rumbling as if saying we were being let off with a warning.

Inside, Mother patted her dampened hair, lady-like, while I, not so lady-like, shook myself off like Sushi after a bath.

Skylar James, wearing his trademark western-style shirt, jeans, and cowboy boots, was arranging leather and silver bolo ties on a spin-display. He looked startled when he saw us, but then most people do.

Approaching, he said, frowning, 'I thought you gals wouldn't be back for another few days.'

'Well, yes,' Mother replied, 'but the best-laid plans of mice and men, you know.' Women, too, apparently.

Skylar looked from her to me and back to her. 'Somethin' go wrong?'

'It's a loooong story, pardner,' she said.

'"A tale told by an idiot,"' I said, quoting Shakespeare, '"full of sound and fury, signifying nothing."'

Mother shot me a murderous look. Skylar didn't know what to make of us. Few do.

'But the good news,' she told our host, 'is that we did make it to the Old Curiosity Shop.'

'Where Mother reneged on the necklace,' I interjected.

'I was getting to that, dear,' she said tersely.

Skylar's frown deepened. 'Mr Westcott changed his mind about buying it?'

'No,' Mother said. 'I told him I'd simply come to adore the lovely lavaliere.'

He blinked. 'The what?'

I gestured to my throat. 'The thing.'

'Oh.' To Mother, he said with a shrug, 'Well, you *did* pay for it . . . Was he put out at all?'

'No, he was quite understanding.' Mother reached into her tote. 'And just to let you know he had no hard feelings, Mr Westcott wanted you to have this for your trouble.'

Mother handed Skylar the wrapped package, and watched him open it.

'How nice,' the man said. 'I'd mentioned to the ol' boy that Angela's into Agatha Christie, and this is her favorite. I must thank him.'

Blame it on jet lag, and the kerfuffle with Tony, but until now I hadn't put together – nor had Mother, judging by her expression – that it had been less than twenty-four hours since Westcott was killed . . . and Skylar had clearly not been informed!

And why *would* he be?

I searched for the words, afraid Mother would beat me tactlessly to the punch.

Which of course, she did, saying, 'I'm afraid thanking the man won't be necessary. Or, for that matter, possible.'

Skylar's eyes rose from the book. 'Why not?'

'Because Mr Westcott is dead, dear. Quite dead.'

Passed on. No more. Ceased to be. Expired and gone to meet his maker . . .

'Stabbed in the chest with a letter opener,' I added, garnering a withering look from Mother.

Skylar's face paled. 'He was *murdered?*'

Mother nodded. 'Apparently the shop had been under surveillance—'

'By MI5,' I said, taking the wind out of her sails. 'And they questioned us as to why we were there, so your name came up. You might get a long-distance call or something.'

Mother's head swiveled toward me – if it had swung around her neck any further, I'd have figured she was possessed.

She uttered, 'Wait . . . in . . . the . . . car.'

'He has a right to know,' I said indignantly, gesturing to the stunned antiques dealer.

'In . . . the . . . car.'

I shrugged. 'OK.'

And left.

About ten minutes later, the passenger door opened and, with some difficulty thanks to her bad knees, Mother climbed in.

Her displeasure with me had not waned.

'I suppose,' she said, staring straight ahead, 'that had I asked you to *talk*, you'd have kept your mouth shut like a sullen child.'

For once Mother was in the right.

I said, 'Sorry. I'm cranky. *You* sit in coach on an international flight next time. How did Skylar react to being connected to an overseas murder case, however peripherally?'

Mother regarded me. 'You were baiting him on *purpose*!'

'Could be. Perhaps I have depths you don't imagine.'

'I'm only peeved because *I* should have thought of that!' she declared. 'Not that I believe Skylar was involved in anything nefarious.'

'Tony says not.'

'And that opinion seems confirmed by my educated reading of our fellow shop owner's reaction. He appeared genuinely upset by the news. After all, he had dealings with the late Mr Westcott.'

I nodded. 'Where to now?'

'I want to call on Ruth Hassler's daughter and son-in-law.'

'OK,' I said with a shrug. 'Do you know where they live?'

She reached into her magician's hat of a tote bag and withdrew a file folder. 'This will tell me . . .'

'Where'd you get that?' I asked suspiciously.

Mother smiled coyly. 'Let's just say it's on loan from a

certain funeral home.' She put a finger to her lips. 'Ned should have known better than to leave me alone in his office when I visited him last.'

Ruth Hassler's daughter and son-in-law had recently moved to Stoneybrook, an upscale enclave on the outskirts of town. On the way, Mother told me what little she knew about the couple: they were in their late thirties, with no kids, and hadn't been on the best of terms with Ruth. Both had quit blue-collar jobs after inheriting Ruth's estate.

I turned into the entrance of Stoneybrook – a marble monument spelling out its name in huge letters – and followed a winding road past expensive homes, each seemingly trying to outdo the other.

'Thar she blows,' Mother said, pointing.

I gazed through the windshield at the three-story, multi-gabled, tan stone manse. 'More like "land ahoy." Wow. Ruth must've been worth a bundle.'

'Which comes as rather a surprise to *me*,' Mother sniffed. Whether she was miffed at Ruth for keeping her wealth well-hidden, or herself for not knowing about it, I couldn't hazard a guess.

Mother's next remark did clear things up a little: 'She never *ever* brought anything to a church potluck but her appetite!'

I shrugged. 'Maybe that's how she got rich – one potluck at a time.' I'd meant that facetiously, but Mother didn't take it that way.

'You got that right!' she said. 'And then she'd scoop her last heaping helpings into Tupperware brought from home!'

I pulled the Fusion into the wide driveway and up to an open three-car garage, within which gleamed a white BMW sedan, a black GMC truck, and a John Deere sit-down lawn mower – all looking as new and fresh as toys on Christmas morning.

I asked Mother, 'Where did all this money come from?'

'Not Ruth's late husband – he had a small insurance agency. But her family had pearl-button loot. And dear Ruth was an only child. So is her daughter.'

As we exited the car, the master of the manor – in torn Harley T-shirt, soiled jeans and sneakers – ambled out between vehicles, wiping his hands on a rag, looking considerably less fresh and showroom-new than the rest of the garage's contents.

Though Mother had said late thirties, Jared Wallace looked ten years older, burly, with a sizable gut, dark hair thinning, face puffy, nose lumpy, dark eyes small and close-set, like a badger.

No good news expected there from Ancestry dot com.

'Yeah?' he said, standing his ground.

'Jared?' Mother asked pleasantly, approaching. 'Vivian Borne. Friend of your late mother-in-law.'

'I know who you are.'

Mother took that as a compliment. 'Many do! . . . Is your better half at home, by chance?'

His frown pulled all his features to the center of his face. 'Whaddya want with Tiffany?'

Mother froze. Apparently, on the drive over, she hadn't figured out what she *did* want with the woman – she'd gotten a little too used to automatically assembling suspect lists, I guess.

I picked up the ball. 'Ah . . . we have something for her.' Ball to Mother.

Who said, 'Something Ruth had given me that she might want to have.'

Interception by Jared, suddenly less hostile. 'I'll take it.'

Recovery by Brandy. 'We didn't bring it along, I'm afraid.'

Pass to Mother down court, and up for a three-pointer. 'Thought we'd see if Tiffany wanted it first.'

Jared thought about that. It took some effort. Then he said, 'OK. Come with me.'

Swish.

We followed the man and his butt crack up a flagstone sidewalk to a wide porch and then through an over-sized etched-glass cherrywood door. The entry was larger than my bedroom, which couldn't have accommodated the cathedral ceiling, mirror-finish wood floors, and grand cherrywood staircase.

To the left, the formal dining room sported a coffered ceiling, white wainscoting, and expensive-looking modern furniture.

To the right yawned a formal living room, tastefully decorated, a large plush Persian rug covering most of the area, a magnificent marble fireplace the focal point.

Jared, who looked like maybe he was the gardener (and a poor hire), said, 'Wait here. Tif's in the kitchen.'

He walked down a wide corridor to the back of the house, footsteps echoing off parquet flooring. Soon we could hear a muffled conversation between the couple, a few of his words quite clear: 'get rid of,' and '*do* it.'

In another moment, the master of the castle returned with his wife in tow.

Tiffany, like her beloved, also appeared older than her years, but not necessarily from the hard-living, hard-drinking lifestyle her husband evinced. Small, thin, with brown hair and a horsey face that could look pretty, she had the kind of weariness that I associate with a browbeaten wife.

Mother, hands clasped before her, said genuinely, 'Dear, I'm so sorry about your mother.'

'Thank you,' she said quietly, Jared looming over her shoulder like a big nasty bird.

'And it pains me that I missed the funeral,' Mother said, adding – and reaching a little I thought, 'which I know must have been well-attended.'

Tiffany nodded. 'Mother had a lot of friends.'

An awkward silence made it clear we weren't wanted past the entryway.

That didn't stop Mother, of course, who trotted out her best ploy. 'My goodness!' she said, putting a palm to her head. 'I'm feeling a bit dizzy! I . . . I think I should sit down.'

My part in this performance was to give her an arm for support, adding with daughterly concern, glancing at our reluctant hostess, 'And perhaps a glass of water?'

'Of course,' Tiffany said, with obvious actual concern. She turned to her husband. 'Jared?'

He scowled and lumbered off.

While our hostess led us into the living room, I continued to support Mother, then gently deposited her on the couch, and sat beside her, turning to her.

'Thank you, Brandy,' she said, patting my knee. Then to Tiffany, 'I'm sorry to be such a burden, dear.'

'Oh, no . . . no,' she responded, mildly bewildered by how quickly she'd become a bystander in her own home. 'Think nothing of it.'

Jared entered with the glass of water, handed it to Mother, and glowered at her as she took a generous gulp.

'Oh, that's *much* better,' Mother enthused, suddenly re-invigorated, if not enough so to leave. 'Still, I'd better sit a spell. Like the *Beverly Hillbillies* theme song says!'

With the pair living in this house, that seemed a little on the nose.

Jared gave his wife a scornful look, as if this invasion were her fault. 'Tif, I have to finish up in the garage. Then we have that boat to look at, hmm?'

Mother waved a hand, 'Oh, don't worry yourself about me. Go, go! We won't keep your wife long.'

He hesitated, then turned on his heels. In a moment, the front door slammed.

'What a lovely home,' Mother exclaimed, looking all around.

'Thank you,' our hostess replied, and settled into a winged-backed chair near us.

I asked, 'Did you do the decorating yourself?' Frankly wondering how that might be possible.

'No,' Tiffany admitted. 'Everything is from the staging when the house was on the market, and Jared – we – decided to purchase it just that way.'

Just how vast *was* the inheritance?

Mother said, her words dripping with semi-real sincerity, 'Ruth was such a lovely person, so considerate, always thinking of others. Once, when I admired something in her home, she insisted I take it. Which is why we are here.'

The 'it' needed to be something from our house, and not the shop, where it might have been seen for sale. Something of value that Mother could give up, but without too much pain.

Her blue Wedgwood china, boxed and forgotten in the attic? Her black, stenciled Hancock chair in the library that nobody ever sat on? Her collection of rare glass insulators gathering dust on a back porch shelf?

'What did my mother give you?' Tiffany asked.

Mother drew herself up. 'A signed serigraph of "Lady in Lace" by Tamara de Lempicka.'

I made a little squawk. That was *mine*, hanging on the wall in my Art Deco bedroom! If that came down, *Mother* would be hanging in its place!

Fortunately, Tiffany shook her head. 'No, please . . . obviously my mother meant for *you* to have it, and so you should.' She paused. 'Plus, I have no memory of whatever that is, due to the fact that she and I haven't . . . hadn't . . . been on very good terms for quite a while, I'm sorry to say.'

Mother said gently, 'Ever since you married Jared, perhaps?'

The woman swallowed. Nodded. Whispered, 'She . . . she thought I was making a mistake.'

What hung in the air was the unasked question, *Did you?*

Instead, Mother asked, 'When was the last time you saw your mother?'

Tiffany shifted in the chair. 'I don't know . . . three, four months ago? When she wouldn't answer my calls or texts, I got worried, and went over to check on her. I have a key.'

'Did Jared have much contact with Ruth?'

A dry laugh. 'They always avoided each other like the plague.'

Mother paused, probably restraining herself from commenting on the use of cliches, then asked, 'Did you know she'd put in a stair-lift?'

'No. I didn't know she'd failed enough to need something like that. Must've been after my last visit.'

Mother said, 'I'm sorry you and she didn't have time to reconcile before her passing.'

Which caused Tiffany to bury her head in her hands; she began to quietly sob.

Mother, fully recovered now, rose and went over, putting a hand on Tiffany's shaking shoulder. 'I, too, had a difficult relationship with my own mother, which went unresolved.'

This was news to me, although my grandmother had died before I was born. The notion that Mother might have been a handful as a child did seem credible.

Mother was asking, 'You've heard of Matilda Tompkins?'

Tilda was Serenity's resident New Age guru. Among her talents and skills was hypnosis, which Mother sometimes used during her investigations.

Tiffany, wiping wet cheeks with a hand, said, 'Oh yes. I took Tilda's course in chakras and auras, and mantras and mudras, and thought it did me some good.'

Mother beamed. 'I just *knew* you were a kindred spirit! I, too, am a devotee of Tilda's.' A pause. 'She's just become an end-of-life doula, you know, and needs participants for her first class, which is being conducted at Dunn's Crematorium.'

Tiffany recoiled. 'Isn't that . . .?'

'Yes, dear, it's where you participate in your own mock funeral ceremony. The experience is supposed to bring clarity to your life.'

And Lord knows Mother could use a little clarity.

She went on with fake sincerity, 'It could give us closure with our own difficult mothers.'

'I . . . I'll think about it,' Tiffany said quietly.

'Please do,' Mother said. 'The session is tomorrow afternoon at one.' She rose. 'And now we'll take our leave.'

At the door, Mother turned to Tiffany. 'I understand that you're having an estate sale at your mother's home on the weekend.'

'Yes.'

'And that there's a preview beforehand tomorrow morning, for a few dealers who will have first dibs on the merchandise?'

Tiffany nodded. 'Yes, mostly a handful from out of town who couldn't come this weekend.'

Mother smiled sweetly. 'I would consider it a great favor if I could attend the preview as well. My daughter and I are the proprietors of the Trash 'n' Treasures shop, as you may know.'

'Well . . . I . . . that might make other local dealers unhappy that they weren't included.' She looked to me for help.

Nope. I kept the same insipid smile going.

Finally, Tiffany said, 'But I guess that would be all right . . .'

'Splendid, dear. Afterward, we can go to Tilda's class!'

In the car, I said, 'You never told me you didn't get along with your mother.'

She shrugged. 'That's because we *did* get along. Two peas in a pod. Well, of course, she could be a tad *theatrical* at times.'

I let that pass. 'Then what are you up to?'

'I believe Tiffany has more to say, but is afraid to in front of her husband. Perhaps Tilda's class will help loosen her up . . . including her tongue.'

'Just don't expect me to participate. I'm not getting in a coffin until I have no choice.'

I was about to start the car when Mother's cell phone sounded. She plucked it out of her pocket and checked the screen.

'It's our editor, Olivia Adams,' Mother whispered, as if the woman might be able to hear us just by ringing.

'Well, you better answer it,' I said, adding, 'And put her on speaker.'

'How do I do that? I'm not some technological wizard!'

I snatched the cell from Mother, pushed some icons, placed the phone in the cup holder between us. 'Hello, Olivia. This is Brandy.'

'*I was so worried about you and Vivian . . . is she there?*'

Good question. Better question: Is she all there?

'Yes,' I said. 'We can both hear you.'

The very feminine, veddy proper British voice asked, '*Are you both all right?*'

Mother leaned over and shouted into the cell. 'We're tickety-boo, luv!'

I closed my eyes.

'And you'll be thrilled to learn,' Mother was saying, 'that we have the makings of our new book well in hand!'

'*What happened? I couldn't get any information from the police.*'

Mother raised a shush finger to her lips, as if the cell could see. 'Sorry dear, very hush, hush – MI5 and all.'

'*MI5! What difficulties did you encounter?*'

'That would be telling. Let's just say the accommodation at HQ could use a lick of paint.'

'*You were actually incarcerated overnight?*'
'Spoiler alert: yes we were! But the rest will have to wait.'
'*Wait for what?*'
'The delightful new book we will write especially for you and deliver on your desk by Royal Mail in record time. Ta!'

And it turned out Mother did have the technological skill to hit the END button.

Her eyes were gleaming, and you really don't want to know what her smile was like.

'I'm sure our contract is secure,' she said. 'We have our new editor right where we want her.'

'Yes,' I said. 'With an ocean between us.'

A Trash 'n' Treasures Tip

A serigraph is a copy of an original made by pushing paint through a silk screen, and holds more value than a lithograph, which simply puts ink to paper. It's a process favored by Andy Warhol, who gave soup cans a lot more fame than just fifteen minutes.

SIX
Carry On Screaming

Dearest readers, you will be pleased and relieved to learn that Vivian is once again at the helm of the ship, steering the U.S.S. *Borne* through dark and troubled waters with nary a lighthouse beacon to assist, and only my cunning and wit to guide me past the deadly reefs. (To counter Brandy's pedestrian prose, I recently took an on-line MasterClass in creative writing from Neil Gaiman! I think it shows, don't you?)

Before continuing, however, I must address a recent unhappy restaurant encounter. At risk of seeming to be harping upon wait staff, please keep in mind that some years ago I was in that noble profession myself, until tripping and depositing a brimming bowl of hot pea soup in a male patron's lap. I am second to none in my admiration for those capable of combining social skills, mathematical dexterity, and memorization in this honorable pursuit. But the latest indignity foisted upon me by one of their contingent strikes me as audaciously presumptuous.

I was having dinner at Serenity's fine French bistro (the name of which is La French Bistro), seated in a padded booth across from a gal pal (I was enjoying my *salade verte au chèvre chaud*, she the *poulet rôti avec sauce à l'estragon*) when our waiter – I will provide no name or description to avoid social media backlash – appeared with an empty tray. Having all but ignored us throughout the meal – save one meager refill of coffee each – he asked, 'Would you like the table cleared?'

As Frannie (my friend's name) and I had finished with our meals, but not our gabfest, I responded graciously, 'Yes, please.' Then – and here's the rub – he waited for us to pass *him* the dirty dishes, silverware, water glasses, and even the crumpled wrappers of our little butter pads. When the dust settled, Frannie and I had cleared the table *for* him! (To be fair, he hadn't said *he* would do it, merely inquiring if we'd like it cleared.)

While I'm on a roll (buttered or otherwise), I have yet another restaurant tale of indignity, which involves a rather new (at least here in the Midwest) policy of a waiter asking, 'How is the first bite?' – usually before you've had the chance to have one!

(*Editor to Vivian*: Perhaps, Madam, it would be best if you could save these editorial comments for another time or even place? Have you ever considered blogging?)

(*Vivian to Editor*: Righto! And thank you for the suggestion, although I personally prefer the permanence of print over the more ephemeral nature of the Net.)

Taking advantage of the nicely cool sunny day, I hopped on my Vespa for the short ride to Ruth Hassler's domicile to attend the nine o'clock preview of her estate's tag sale.

The house, a Tudor-style, was located near Serenity's downtown in an area that had once been prime real estate, but over the years slowly and steadily declined. Most of these homes, built in the first part of the last century, were large, three-story structures; while not as grand as the city founders' mansions on West Hill, these residences had at the time been considered a satisfactory alternative for those who had acquired considerable money, if not quite enough to be rolling in it.

Unfortunately, over the years these fine if somewhat lesser houses had proved expensive to repair, not conducive to such upgrades as air-conditioning with its extensive duct-work. In addition, these abodes had been routinely overlooked by historical preservation groups whose grant money went to restoring and maintaining Serenity's grander old structures.

When I arrived, cars were already crowding the curb, so I zipped up the cracked driveway and parked my trusty Vespa off to one side. As I approached the front porch, a man and woman I didn't recognize (surely not locals, as my knowledge of my fellow Serenity citizenry is second to none) were coming out the door, the man grumbling to his companion, 'Not worth the trip.'

Well, that just meant more goodies for me, didn't it?

Inside, the clutter for which Ruth was notorious had been hidden or hauled away, the crème-de-la-crème furnishings nicely arranged, though on closer inspection they seemed more two-percent milk than cream. About a dozen dealers were circling around in their loping bird of prey manner, examining the merchandise and price tags; more of these predators would be upstairs, I assumed.

I spotted the owner of the tag sale company, Michael Hughes, who was handling the event, and – as we were well known to each other – approached him with a smile.

The middle-aged auction-house man gave the appearance of a distinguished college professor, sporting wire-framed glasses, a well-trimmed beard, a three-piece brown tweed suit, and his trademark argyle socks.

With his infectious smile, and deeply resonant voice, Michael had rapidly expanded his Iowa City-based business to outlying areas, chiefly by undercutting the competition, taking the lowest percentage of sales in eastern Iowa.

'Vivian,' Michael said, an amused twinkle in his eye, 'I *thought* you might wrangle an invite.'

'You know me all too well, dear.'

Which he did, having once offered to combine our businesses, and *more* than once to merge not just our company names. But somehow I just couldn't see myself darning argyle socks.

I said, 'I'm a bit surprised you took this one on.'

He gave me *that* smile, the one that meant business but not the antiques business, if you know what I mean. Let's just say it conveyed a certain charm, making me wonder if I'd made a mistake spurning him. After all, a girl could always just discreetly buy *new* argyles . . .

'Viv, you know my motto,' he said. 'Every estate has its rewards.' Then he leaned in to whisper, 'But I may regret the time that went into this one.' He straightened and his voice returned to a normal level. 'On the other hand – did you know *Colette Dumont* made the trip down here?'

I sucked in air. '*Do* tell!'

He nodded, gestured toward the back. 'Last I saw her, she was in the kitchen.'

I had long wanted to meet the elusive, still-single lady, who owned an upscale antiques shop, also in Iowa City, but seemed to spend much of her time abroad. The few opportunities I'd had to drive to her store in hopes of catching her there – back when I had my driver's license, of course (as far as you, and Brandy, know) – I'd invariably been greeted by an underling.

'What's on offer here,' Michael said, 'seems a trifle mundane for the likes of Colette herself Dumont. What does she know that we don't know, Vivian?'

'Probably a good number of things, my dear.'

'No argument there.'

'As nice as it is to see you,' I said, quietly, 'can we suspend the chitchat till I've had a chance to get a look around? Much of the competition has beaten me to the punch already.'

He gave me that smile again. 'I understand – the thrill of the hunt. I should circulate, anyway, myself. One client leads to another, after all.'

I patted his arm, then made a beeline for the kitchen, on the way spotting Skylar talking to Ruth's son-in-law, Jared Wallace. Skylar was in his typical western wear, if a little spiffier than usual, though Jared was strictly Harley T-shirt and old jeans. So I wasn't the only townie interloper among the out-of-town dealers.

The legendary Colette was seated at an oaken table, an example of modern early American style, certainly too gauche for la Grande Dame Dumont to be interested in. As she held court, other dealers gathered around her, standing behind chairs they dared not take themselves.

This was a rare public appearance, after all. Colette was a unicorn among horses, not to mention a few jackasses.

I could only admire her poise and beauty, reluctant though those feelings were. She was an extremely well-conserved fifty, her lovely Elizabeth Taylor-like face due to excellent genes perhaps, or maybe a skilled plastic surgeon (possibly both – I wonder who hers was?), her chin-length bob black and sleek, her attire expensive, most likely Parisian couture.

Colette was saying, 'And then when my father died, I took over his business, though I had not an *iota* of knowledge about antiques. My indoctrination came rather quickly when I let a Ming Dynasty vase go for less than half its value, not realizing the rarity.' A musical laugh. 'I never made such an abecedarian mistake again – about *anything*.'

Titters and grins all around. I was not grinning, however – her pretentious manner of speech I found insufferable!

'Would you like some coffee, Ms Dumont?' Tiffany interjected. The late Ruth's daughter had been standing apart from the group near a coffee station, sipping from a ceramic mug with a kitty on it.

Colette gave her a warm smile. 'It does smell delicious, Tiffany. But I must decline. I monitor my caffeine carefully.'

Not one to stand on the sidelines, I muscled my way to the table to ask bluntly, 'You're well known for your shop, Ms Dumont. But don't you operate as a *picker*, as well? Does that explain why you've honored us with your presence?'

Her violet eyes turned to me. 'You're Vivian Borne, aren't you?' Which was presented more as a statement, than question. A slender, manicured hand never introduced to dishwater came toward me.

I extended one that knew dishwater well, and we shook. Legend meets legend.

'In the flesh,' I said.

Releasing my hand, she enthused, not just to me but to the dealers paying her homage, 'I've long been wanting to meet the gifted Mrs Borne!' Then, to me, she said, 'I've admired your talents ever since I trekked to the Serenity Community Theater and witnessed your artistry in *You Can't Take It With You*.'

Good Lord! I hoped that wasn't the performance where I accidentally set the curtains ablaze after insisting on using real fireworks.

Colette went on, 'In my opinion, your portrayal of the Grand Duchess Olga surpassed Elizabeth Ashley's in the Broadway revival of some years ago.'

I'd thought so, too, even though I had never actually seen that performance. But I half-bowed and did a roll of my hand as if addressing a sultana, and demurred, 'How kind of you.'

I had obviously misjudged this woman. She was clearly a creature of exquisite taste and perception.

'And, of course,' she went on, 'you are equally adept as an author. When traveling, I always download your latest mystery on my tablet, and . . . if I'm not overstepping to say so . . . I find the chapters you've written yourself far more compelling, far better-written, than those of your daughter's, however well-meaning a child she might be.'

Such discerning taste!

(*Note to Mother from Brandy*: She didn't say that last part.)

(*Note to Brandy from Mother*: Are you calling me a liar?)

(*Note to Mother from Brandy*: Very perceptive, Mother. And discerning.)

(*Note to Vivian and Brandy from Editor*: Ladies, I must insist that you please settle this matter before we go to the proof stage. Corrections then!)

(*Mother and Brandy*: Always.)

I began, 'Ms Dumont—'

'*Please* . . . call me Colette. And might I call you Vivian? . . . Good. Thank you.' Her smile was dazzling. 'I feel as though we're going to be great friends.'

What an honor!

'But Colette,' I began, 'if you might answer my question? Which in retrospect I believe may have been indelicately phrased.'

'Not at all, Vivian. You are correct. I do act as a, shall we say, "personal shopper" for certain select clients – but "picker" is such a vulgar word, don't you think?'

'I do,' I said, but I didn't really. I always thought 'vulgar' sounded just like what it described.

She continued: 'As a seasoned globe-trotter, I have found that adding the service arrow to my quiver, so to speak, is beneficial to business.' She leaned forward with an amused smile and all but whispered, 'After all, it makes travel deductible.'

What a clever woman!

Vivian Borne, I told myself, *you've never misjudged anyone so thoroughly.*

Colette pushed back her chair and stood; unlike Liz Taylor, she was tall and slender as well as lovely.

'And now I must go,' the esteemed antiques dealer pronounced. 'I have an auction to attend this afternoon.' The crowd parted, Red Sea-like, as she crossed over to Tiffany, granting her a smile.

'Has my purchase been loaded into my car, Mrs Wallace?'

Tiffany, who appeared intimidated by the sudden close proximity to the woman – as if in the presence of royalty – responded, 'Yes, Ms Dumont. Jared has already taken care of it.'

That justified wearing T-shirt and jeans to his late mother-in-law's tag sale – not that I figured he'd have dressed any differently in other circumstances.

Tiffany concluded the exchange: 'And thank you for coming, Ms Dumont.'

'Most happy to.'

Colette departed, leaving behind a gaggle of admirers, myself included, frankly. I'd been *so* wrong about her.

I wandered back into the living room, looking for something to buy to justify my presence without it costing much. In the process of doing so, I bumped into a woman I recognized as Skylar's wife, Angela – *literally* bumped into her. We had never formally met, though I'd seen her once at The Trading Post, dropping something off to her husband.

After apologizing for not looking where I was going – I do get distracted on murder cases, even just potential ones – I introduced myself, and said, 'You and your husband have such an interesting shop. A very nice addition to Serenity's antiquing family.'

'Thank you, Mrs Borne.' She was a dark-haired, curvy beauty as compared to her fair-haired, slender husband, lending credence to the adage that opposites attract. 'But I'm hardly ever there. I stick to teaching.'

'Skylar did mention that.' I cocked my head. 'Then I'm surprised you were able to attend the preview this morning.'

'Spring break.'

'Ah! A godsend to both students *and* teachers.'

'I'm only along in case Skylar buys something and needs help loading and unloading.' She smiled, said, 'Nice to meet you,' and moved on.

A collection of Snowbabies figurines arranged on an accent table near the front window caught my eye. While examining them, I happened to glance outside. At the curb, standing next to a silver Jaguar, Colette was speaking to Skylar. Since his back was to me, and she was blocked by him, I could draw no conclusions about the conversation.

I kept examining the figurines until Colette got into her expensive ride and drove off, while Skylar returned inside.

'You've met Ms Dumont before?' I asked as he was passing by.

'Never had the pleasure,' he said, with just a touch of western drawl and a sideways smile. 'Nice gal. Knowledgeable, too. Pardon.'

And he kept moving.

Having no reason to extend my stay further, I selected a Snowbaby, paid one of Michael's minions for it at a table near the front door, and returned to the kitchen to remind Tiffany of Tilda's one o'clock death class.

Upon entering, I found the recently crowded kitchen now empty but for two people: Ruth's daughter in the arms of Skylar. My, this cowboy *did* get around! Not his first time at the rodeo . . .

'Pardon *me*!' I said, and began to back out.

'Oh . . . Mrs Borne,' Tiffany said, extracting herself from the young man, her eyes red and a little puffy. 'It's . . . not what it looks like.'

'None of my business, I'm sure.' Admittedly, that's not something I often say.

She went on: 'I didn't think the sale would affect me so much, and Mr James just happened to be the nearest shoulder to cry on.'

'It's a nice enough shoulder,' I said.

Skylar asked Tiffany sympathetically, 'Would you like me to get Jared for you?'

'No!' she responded sharply. Then, softer, 'I'll be all right. It just . . . took me by surprise, is all. The rush of emotions.'

I asked, 'Why don't we sit down and I'll keep you company a while. Maybe you can have some coffee and relax a bit.'

My offer was accepted, and – as I led Tiffany to the oak table – Skylar slipped out.

'Don't berate yourself, my dear,' I said, once she and I had settled. 'Your mother was a trying woman, self-centered, boorish, and rude. But that doesn't lessen the loss, does it?'

Always adept at consoling, with a peerless instinct of just what to say, I seldom need to speak but a few sentences before the troubled person claims to feel better now, and that I needn't say more.

'I'm all right, Mrs Borne,' Tiffany responded.

I rest my case.

But I continued, 'Because of your relationship with this diffi-cult woman, I think it's vitally important that you attend Tilda's session this afternoon, so you might finally confront your feel-ings, and put them to rest.' So to speak. 'Otherwise, they'll fester like a boil, growing larger and larger, only to burst later, when you least expect it, projecting purulence all over everything.'

Thank you, Neil Gaiman!

She nodded slowly. 'You're right.'

'Perhaps it would be helpful if we went together.' I didn't want her backing out at the last minute.

And if you're thinking that my attempts at consolation were actually just an effort to manipulate her into attending that class of Tilda's, well, don't you think I'm capable of doing two things at once?

'Thank you, Mrs Borne, but I have my car, and I'll leave from here after the sale.'

I stood. 'Then I'll see you at Dunn's at one. Oh! And you'll need to bring a framed photo of yourself.'

I gathered my small purchase and exited the kitchen. On my way out the front door, Skylar and Angela were on the porch in the midst of what appeared to be a tense, no, *intense* conver-sation, which abruptly ceased upon seeing my shining face.

Could the couple have been fighting over Tiffany?

Could Tiffany have been leaning on more of Skylar than just a shoulder?

Seated around a table in a meeting room at the Dunn funeral home, and ready to participate in Tilda's first session as a death doula, were six people: myself; Frannie (my aforementioned friend and a former nurse); Vern, a retired chiropractor and member of the ROMEOS group (Retired Old Men Eating Out); Norma Crumley, Serenity's foremost socialite and president of the local League of Women Voters; and two college-age girls, possibly here for a lark, or perhaps with genuine New Age leanings.

Thus far, Tiffany was a no-show.

Tilda, wearing her usual bohemian attire – white blouse with voluminous sleeves, long patchwork skirt, Birkenstock sandals – stood before a large blackboard. Exuding an aura of peace and calm, Tilda was a slender forty-something with long golden-red hair, translucent skin, and a scattering of youthful freckles across the bridge of her nose.

The guru addressed the class.

'For those who don't know me, I'm Matilda Tompkins – but everyone calls me Tilda.' She paused with a somber smile. 'I want to thank you for participating in the first session of "Appreciating Life Through Death," which will be a new experience for all of us, myself included.'

The door opened, and Tiffany rushed in, looking a little flushed; she was carrying the requested framed photo of herself (Tilda had collected ours earlier) and slipped into the nearest empty chair. We locked eyes, and I smiled reassuringly.

Heads swiveled back to Tilda, who continued: 'What does a death doula do? Many assist in the dying process, helping families cope with the passing of a loved one by recognizing it as a natural process.

'Others work directly with the dying person, caring for their physical, emotional, and spiritual needs. They are, however, as I am, non-medical professionals – that is to say, not trained in the medical field – and prescribe no medicines.

'It's important to understand that death doulas – or end-of-life doulas – are relatively new to America, and represent an ever-evolving field.

'I restrict myself to the area of spirituality and enlightenment of the living, to reintroduce joy back into the lives of those whose existence has become joyless, whether through hardship or hard-heartedness. And to remind them that life *will come to an end*, so they should make the most of the time they have left.'

My mind began to wander (as perhaps yours has, too).

Was Tiffany having an affair with Skylar, as was my initial impression?

'My approach is nature-based, supported by psychopomp, with a heavy dose of shaman . . .'

What was the conversation that passed between Skylar and Colette?

'In a repressed society that avoids dealing with death, it's important to become comfortable with it, to understand the natural conclusion of life . . .'

Could that really have been the first time Skylar met Colette?

'To that end – pun definitely intended – I've taken a ceremonial approach, where my students will have an opportunity not only to confront death, but also detox emotionally, and reflect on how precious life is.'

What had Skylar and Angela been discussing?

'When this class is over, I hope that each of you will have a new outlook on life, and no longer harbor a fear of death.'

And, finally, had I selected the right Snowbaby?

'In order to simulate your funeral – or *living* funeral, if you like – Mr Dunn has been gracious enough to provide the coffins—'

Norma Crumley interrupted: 'We're not getting *inside* them, are we?'

'Yes,' Tilda answered. 'I thought you understood the nature of this class.'

'Not *that* part!' the socialite exclaimed. 'And we're certainly not going to slide into the . . . the . . .'

'Crematorium itself? No. The coffins are positioned on the floor nearby and will remain there.' The guru put a finger to her lips. 'Although, in future, that might be a nice touch – furnace off, of course.'

Norma persisted. 'Surely the lids won't be closed!'

'Just for ten minutes,' Tilda said.

And don't call me 'Shirley!' Isn't Airplane *just the funniest film?*

Tilda was saying, 'Closing them for that long will give you time to reflect upon—'

Standing abruptly, Norma announced, 'No *thank* you.'

In another moment she was gone.

Tilda, seemingly nonplussed, asked, 'Anyone else unclear on the procedure? Or would like to reconsider?' A pause. 'You must trust in the ceremony – otherwise, having me just stand here lecturing you on how to better appreciate life won't be nearly as powerful or effective.'

Silence.

Another somber smile from Tilda. 'Excellent. And now, as a symbolic gesture, each of you will write a brief will.' She began to pass out paper and pens. 'Don't worry, it's not a real document. Not legally binding in the least.'

While we performed this rather ghoulish task (to some, not me; I in jest left all my worldly goods to Sushi), Tilda took the photo Tiffany had brought, and slipped out of the room.

When the death doula came back, she collected our papers.

'Now,' Tilda said, 'we'll proceed to another room that I've prepared . . . There are restrooms along the way.'

I don't know why she looked at me when she said that! Do I have an animated pink cartoon bladder following me around, like in that commercial?

But just to be safe, I did duck into the Ladies', just in case nature might be lurking, ready to call. Before you head into the desert, it's wise to stop at LAST CHANCE GAS, and not just for fuel.

When I'd caught up to the others, they had gathered in front of a closed door labeled CREMATORIUM. Tiffany, who suddenly moved next to me, whispered, 'I need to talk to you.' She had a hand on her stomach – probably nervous about what was to come.

'Don't be afraid, dear,' I said reassuringly, 'to face your inner feelings.'

'No. Not about this.' She frowned. She didn't seem irritated – more . . . tormented.

'We'll go out for coffee and have a nice long chat, afterward,' I suggested.

Tiffany nodded.

Good. If Tilda's process proved traumatizing or even uplifting to Tiffany, I might well get more out of the young woman. I wasn't really here to learn about how to deal with anybody's death but her late mother's, after all.

Tilda was saying, 'This is a sacred room, and shall be treated as such. There's nothing "funny" about it to spread around on social media.' She was looking at the two young college-aged girls, who cast their eyes downward.

'All right,' Tilda said. 'Inside, there are seven stations. Please find yours, which is identified with your photo, and wait for further instruction.'

We entered solemnly, as if going into a chapel.

The large room was blindingly white with touches of gleaming stainless steel. (I'd been inside this chamber before, while acting as sheriff, to stop the cremation of a man I suspected had been murdered, halting the procedure just before the body entered the furnace.) (*Antiques Fire Sale.*)

At the back was a roller belt that would move the deceased inextricably along in a plain wooden coffin of inferior wood (why burn the good stuff?) and into the hot chamber's wide mouth with its fangs of flames. But, at the moment, the belt was silent, the hungry mouth closed, temporarily satiated.

(*Note from Editor to Vivian*: Madam, perhaps you'd like to soften the above paragraph, which some might consider quite disturbing.)

(*Vivian to Editor*: With all due respect, our readers are quite used to being disturbed. But you must admit – isn't that MasterClass paying off?)

Spread out on the tiled floor were seven of these plain coffins, each accompanied by a small squat table that held our photos, along with a single long-stemmed white calla lily, and a small aromatic candle, flickering.

No one balked. We moved to our places – Tiffany's coffin was next to mine – and waited as instructed.

'Enter your casket and lie down,' Tilda said.

We did. The wooden bottom was hard, but there was a little satin pillow on which to lay our weary heads. Wouldn't have minded one of those for at home in bed to prop the ol' noggin up while reading!

As Tilda began to float among us like a friendly apparition, soft music began to play 'Clair de Lune' by Debussy. (If you're not familiar with the classic, take a break and listen to it on the Net, so you can get the proper soundtrack going in your head. I'll wait.)

'Breathe slowly in and out,' our doula directed. 'Clear any thoughts from your mind. Use this time for personal reflection, to forgive yourself for past mistakes, to forgive others for theirs, and to contemplate my earlier words to create a better, more fulfilling life going forward.'

Tilda continued her ethereal movements.

'I'm now going to close each casket for ten minutes,' she announced, adding, 'If, at any time you become uncomfortable, the lid can easily be opened by yourself . . . but please remain reclined within.'

Suddenly I was in darkness, except for a few shafts of light entering through several small holes. I found it quite pleasant, actually, the air filling with the scent of the candles, music wafting in.

What was it Tiffany wanted to tell me? I wondered.

I am embarrassed to say that I'm afraid I fell asleep. The experience was surprisingly restful. I was awoken by the voice of God, gently whispering, 'Vivian . . .'

And God was a woman!

Actually, it was just Tilda.

'Please wake up, Vivian,' the voice above the coffin lid said quietly. 'You're snoring. It's disturbing the process for everyone else.'

But then she was gone, although soon something else, *someone* else, disturbed the process far more than had my gentle sawing of logs.

Muffled screams!

Coming from quite near me!

Throwing open my lid, I determined the cries of distress were coming from Tiffany's coffin, and I clambered out of mine – as quickly as a person with two hip replacements and bad knees can clamber, anyway.

By the time I got there the screams had stopped.

I threw open her lid.

Her face wore a frozen look of terror, mouth open, but no longer functioning, eyes wide, but not seeing.

As if she'd been frightened to death.

Vivian's Trash 'n' Treasures Tip

When deciding upon the method of disposing of an estate, tag sales are becoming more popular than auctions. Tag sales are usually held over a three-day period, giving buyers more flexibility to attend, as compared to an auction set on a certain day with undetermined prices on the items. The last auction I went to, I waited around all day only to be out-bid for a genuine autographed photo of Clark Gable.

SEVEN
Carry On Doctor

B randy back at the helm of the U.S.S. *Borne*, just in time to guide the ship off the shoals.

Confused by all these characters? Me too. So here's a list of everyone you've met so far, in order of their appearance, who will continue to be viable:

Mother
Me
Sushi
Dumpster Dan
Tony Cassato, Serenity Chief of Police
Rocky, Tony's dog (and love of Sushi's life)
Ned Dunn, funeral home owner/director
Ruth Hassler, Tiffany's deceased mother
Renny, Cinders' bar owner
Nona, tupla (and her imaginary friend Zelda)
Skylar James, owner of The Trading Post antique shop
Angela James, grade-school teacher, Skylar's wife
Humphrey Westcott, the Old Curiosity Shop manager
MI5 Agent Hasty
Tiffany Wallace
Jared Wallace, Tiffany's husband
Michael Hughes, tag sale firm proprietor
Colette Dumont, Iowa City antiques dealer

And an honorable mention goes to Trash 'n' Treasures assistant Joe Lange, who you'll never really meet.

Banish all others from your mind. Tilda Tompkins, for example, is not a suspect. And Mother didn't do it, and I didn't do it, and Sushi didn't do it – you're not reading Agatha Christie here!

Remember that old expression, you can't tell the players without a scorecard? Well, now you have a scorecard. Never mind the players on the bench, and pay no attention to that man behind the curtain.

(*Mother to Brandy*: You are mixing metaphors again, dear. Really, you must enroll in that creative writing MasterClass!)

And stay alert. You'll be on your own from here on out. (But, to assist you, I will add an asterisk to the names of new non-essential characters.)

Look at it this way. When you're playing a round of Clue, you better have all the game pieces at hand.

At around three in the afternoon, I was behind the counter at the shop, which was otherwise unoccupied except for Sushi, when a call came in on my cell.

Mother.

'Dear,' she said. 'There's been a little snafu at Tilda's class.'

'What class?'

'"Appreciating Life Through Death," which I attended this afternoon. Do keep up, dear.'

'. . . OK.'

'Don't you pay attention to *anything* I tell you?'

'What?'

A sound somewhere between a grunt and growl came from the phone. 'Keep in mind what Charlie Chan once said, young lady – "willful child soon find self out of will."'

'He said no such thing. Where are you, anyway?'

'The hospital.'

I straightened. 'Are you all right?'

'Well, my hammer toes are throbbing, and thank you for asking, but otherwise I'm fine, dear. It's Tiffany Wallace who has an issue.'

'What kind of issue?'

'She's fighting for her life after the paramedics managed to revive her.'

Now she had my eyes popping. 'What *happened*?'

'Not exactly sure. Perhaps a panic attack got out of hand and turned into a heart attack. Not everyone reacts well to being put in a coffin.'

I looked at the phone.

It said to me, 'Perhaps you'd better come to the ER, dear. All will be revealed.'

She clicked off, and I suppose I could have called her back, but instead I just shut down the computer, brought in the flags, scooped up Sushi, set the alarm, and headed out.

In the hospital parking lot, I left the little furball in the car (window cracked), then at the ER was directed by a nurse to one of the small private waiting rooms reserved for families of serious cases.

I went quickly in only to find Tony poised between Mother and Jared, the chief bodily blocking Tiffany's husband, whose verbal attacks were threatening to become physical.

'This is *your* fault!' Jared was yelling at Mother. 'If Tiffany hadn't gone to that stupid class, she wouldn't be in a *coma* right now!'

'Take it easy, Mr Wallace,' Tony said evenly. 'As I understand it, your wife took that class on her own accord.'

'But it was *her* idea,' the distressed man responded, waggling an accusatory finger past the chief at Mother, who stood placidly with arms folded. 'I'm going to *sue* her, *and* that screwball woman who ran the class!'

Rarely did Mother share a sentence with another individual and not be the one labeled a screwball.

A doctor I recognized as Param Singh appeared in the doorway; he'd taken care of me in the ER last fall after Mother accidently Tased me while she was testing out a new gizmo. (*Antiques Frame.*)

'Mr Wallace,' Dr Singh said gently, approaching the man, 'perhaps we should talk alone.'

Jared took a step back. 'She's . . . she's gone, isn't she? Dead.'

A somber Singh nodded. 'I'm sorry . . . we did everything we could.'

Tiffany's husband sank into a nearby chair. He hunkered over, staring at the floor, knees apart, folded hands hanging.

'I can't believe it,' he said. 'Just . . . just yesterday we were shopping for a boat . . . looking forward to spending this summer out on the river . . .'

The doctor said, 'Mr Wallace, I'm going to have to order an autopsy.'

Jared looked up at him sharply. 'What?'

'An autopsy.'

'*Why?* Tiffany had a heart attack, didn't she?' Jared shot Mother a murderous glance. 'After being shut inside a *coffin*!'

'There's no indication of a heart attack,' Singh told him, 'although that remains a possibility. In any case, sir, we are legally required to determine the cause of death.'

Jared got to his feet, eyes blazing. 'Tiffany's *gone*! What the hell *difference* does it make *what* killed her!'

'A great deal,' Singh said quietly. 'To the state board, and to myself, as the attending physician when she was brought in.'

'Well,' Jared said indignantly, 'I won't give you my permission.'

'Actually I don't need your permission, Mr Wallace,' the doctor replied. 'I'm merely informing you that an autopsy will be performed.'

Tony turned to the doctor. 'A word?'

Singh nodded, and the two professionals stepped out of the little room and shut us in.

Again Mother and I looked at each other. A forced autopsy meant only one thing: Tiffany's death had been deemed officially suspicious. Her nod to me was barely perceptible, but it said: *We are in this.*

And we were.

Jared sat down again, then said to no one in particular, 'I just can't bear the thought of Tiff being . . . being cut up like that.'

Mother pulled another chair over next to him. 'Dear? May I give you some advice?'

I steeled myself. Mother had what some would see as a cold-blooded view of people dying, but I knew she took nothing more seriously than murder. Her duty, as she saw it, was to the deceased, for whom syrupy sorrow did nothing at all. And to the grieving by providing closure.

But she could come across as tactless. You probably have already noticed that.

Jared swiveled toward her, sneering. 'And *why* would I take advice from you?'

'Because doing so is in your best interest.'

Something in Mother's voice must have caused him to take her seriously.

'I'm listening,' he said.

'When the doctor returns,' she said, 'you should freely offer to sign the autopsy form.'

Jared looked at her like she was crazy – she got that a lot, actually. He spread his hands. 'You heard the man – he's going to do it *anyway*, so what difference does it make?'

'A great deal,' Mother replied, adding, 'where your defense is concerned.'

Jared frowned. '*What* defense?'

'Unless I'm wrong – and I seldom am in such matters – when the autopsy report comes back, Chief Cassato will be looking at you as the main person of interest, if not the prime suspect.'

'Suspect in *what*?' he asked acidly, not understanding.

'Why, the killing of your wife, of course.'

Jared's eyes widened, any defiance in his manner evaporating. 'She was . . . *murdered*?'

Mother nodded. 'That's a conclusion to which the doctor and, I venture to say, our chief of police have already come. Why else would an autopsy be required? Your signature on the form will look better for you in court.'

His reply came out a pitiful squawk: 'But . . . but I didn't kill her!'

Mother shrugged. 'Perhaps not, Mr Wallace. But someone certainly did. And the spouse is the first person police look at. And often the last.'

The door opened, the physician returning alone.

Jared jumped to his feet. 'Doctor! I've decided to authorize the autopsy. I'll make no effort to fight it. I want to do everything I can to help determine the cause of Tiffany's death.'

'Wise decision, Mr Wallace,' Singh said, and crooked a finger. 'Come with me.'

They left.

'We're in it,' I said to Mother.

She smiled. 'To win it!'

Well, at least she waited for the murdered woman's husband to leave before letting tactlessness take over.

In the parking lot, we caught up with Tony as he was about to get into his unmarked car.

Mother, out of breath, asked, 'Well?'

He turned to her wearing the kind of face you usually see carved on a totem pole. 'Well what?'

'Let's not waste each other's time,' she replied congenially. 'I'll have a copy of that autopsy report two minutes after it's filed with the coroner.'

Tony's steel-gray eyes went to me.

I nodded, shrugged. 'She's got a mole in his office.'

His sigh began at his toes. 'Oh . . . kay, Vivian. What do you want to know exactly?'

'What assumptions are you and the doctor making? What does Dr Singh think is the cause of Tiffany's death?'

This second sigh only started at his chest. 'Probably poison.'

'I *thought* so!' Mother exclaimed gleefully. Her brow furrowed. 'But we had no refreshments during Tilda's class. I suppose it's possible Tiffany might have had a lozenge or piece of candy tucked away in a pocket – none of us girls took our purses into the coffins.'

I wondered if that last sentence had ever been spoken by a human before in the history of mankind.

The chief said, 'She might have been dosed with something slow-acting.'

'Ahhh,' Mother said slowly. 'I did see her clutching her stomach, but merely attributed that to nerves.'

She turned away from Tony to me. 'You weren't there, dear, but plenty of possible suspects presented themselves at the tag sale this morning, and Tiffany had been drinking coffee from a particular cup.' She began ticking off her fingers. 'Husband Jared, of course, who would inherit all their money. Skylar James, who may have been having an affair with Tiffany. And even Colette Dumont, who – judging by the unimpressive goods on hand – had no discernible reason to be there, and—'

I cleared my throat, and Mother caught herself, finally, clamping her jabber jaws.

'Thank you, Vivian, for the information,' Tony said with a tiny smile.

Mother practically begged, 'I'm obviously cooperating with you – give me something in return!'

The chief was opening his car door. 'Such as?'

'Where was Jared when he got word of this?'

Tony shrugged. 'The late Ruth Hassler's residence, cleaning up after the sale.' Climbing in behind the wheel, he said over his shoulder, 'Michael Hughes confirms that Jared was there right up to being called to the hospital.'

He started the engine, nodded to me, and we stepped aside as the car backed out. We stood watching him drive away.

'You could've found that out easily,' I said. 'Kind of a wasted question, if you thought Tony owed you something in return.'

'That's all I could think of to ask,' she grumbled. 'He had me at a disadvantage! Once I start counting clues on my fingers, I'm off to the races.'

Tony getting the best of Mother was a rare occurrence.

'Let's go home,' I said. 'Little girl, you've had a busy day.'

'I am bushed,' Mother admitted.

She headed for her Vespa, and I to my Fusion.

Arriving at the house first, I set Sushi down in the foyer, where she suddenly took off, running around the living room, nose sniffing the floor, ears perked, giving out with a low, suggestive growl.

Mother, upon coming in the front door and seeing me frozen in the entryway, asked, 'What is it?'

'We've had a visitor,' I said.

This was hardly the first time our home had been burgled. When you go messing in murder, the people responsible for the crime get interested in you. But this was the first time we'd been 'visited' in broad daylight.

'Bold,' Mother responded, complimenting the audacity of our unknown intruder. 'I'll take the high road, dear, and you take the low road.'

At least she didn't sing it.

As Mother climbed the stairs, I moved slowly through the

living room, then the kitchen, followed by the dining room, where I opened drawers and cupboards and closets, looking for anything missing or even just disturbed.

I had just finished searching the library/music room when Mother joined me.

'Anything?' I asked her.

'My jewelry box had been opened and gone through, but everything seems to be there.'

I'd talked her into keeping the good stuff in a safe deposit box at the bank.

'What about you?' she asked.

A shake of my head. 'I wouldn't have suspected a thing if it weren't for Sushi.'

'Our good little bloodhound.' Mother grunted. 'Would appear we had a gentleman burglar.'

'Who didn't want the police called,' I surmised. 'With nothing missing and no sign of forced entry, we can hardly ask for fingerprinting.'

'Probably used lock picks to get in through the back door,' Mother observed.

She should know.

I said, 'The only thing missing is a book from the shelf.' I pointed to the empty spot. Mother's favorite mystery novels were there and arranged in a special way that made the missing tooth in the shelf's smile easy to spot.

'No, dear, that's where I kept my copy of the Christie book, before giving it to Skylar.'

'Oh, right,' I said, then frowned. 'Where's that necklace you bought from him?'

'In my bag.' She snapped her fingers. 'That's what the burglar was looking for!'

'And couldn't find,' I said, nodding.

'I'd meant to take it to the jeweler to examine.'

Excitement was building!

I said, 'Let's examine it ourselves.'

She retrieved the jewelry, brought it into the dining room, and placed the necklace on the Duncan Phyfe table beneath the Art Nouveau hanging light fixture.

We leaned in and looked.

'What if,' Mother said slowly, 'the stones aren't really turquoise, but are only painted to look as such?'

I was skeptical. 'And what? Beneath are diamonds or other precious gems?'

'Get the paint remover,' she ordered.

The door to the basement was in the kitchen, and I clomped down the stairs, located the paint-remover can, got a rag, and returned.

Meanwhile, Mother had spread a towel beneath the necklace on the table. I handed her the remover, and she poured some on the cloth. After selecting the largest stone, Mother began to rub.

And rub.

Nothing.

I asked, 'What if the precious stones are *inside* the outer layer?'

Mother straightened. '*The* hammer, dear,' she said dramatically.

We only had one.

In the kitchen was a drawer of tools designated for small household fixes – hammer, screwdrivers (long and short), pliers (slip joint, needle nose), wire cutter, and wrench; plus an assortment of nails, screws, bolts, picture frame hangers, carpet tacks, and unidentified hardware found beneath furniture we thought we ought to keep – the kind of items that seemed to breed when we weren't looking.

But the hammer wasn't there.

I returned with the bad news.

'Where did you use it last?' Mother asked.

'I didn't,' I said.

'*I* always put it back,' she sniffed.

I arched an eyebrow. 'Do you now. Care to wager a little bet?'

Mother threw her head back. 'Name your terms.'

'The loser makes dinner,' I said, adding, '*And* cleans up after.'

Mother put a finger to her lips. 'On second thought, I may have used it in my bedroom to fix a closet shelf.'

Usually, duct tape was her first go-to fixer. Her second was Old School epoxy clue.

'Be a dear, will you?' Mother asked. 'You know how hard the stairs are on my knees.'

When I returned with the hammer, Mother held out a hand as if requesting a scalpel – my memory jumped to Moe of the Three Stooges as a surgeon asking Larry for gibberish medical instruments – with the necklace laid out on the table, awaiting her skilled surgical touch.

WHAM!

The turquoise remained intact.

Her next blow rattled the windows, and the stone broke apart in pieces, revealing . . .

. . . nothing.

'Pulverized,' I commented.

Mother looked at me sourly. 'Any *other* bright ideas?'

'*You* asked for the hammer.'

'*You* should have stopped me. Now my necklace is ruined! It travels to London and back, safe and sound, and in one moment in Serenity, you *destroy* it!'

I squinted one eye. 'Have you had your medicine?'

She squinted one eye. 'Have you had *yours*?'

Come to think of it, I had missed this morning's Prozac.

Mother snapped out of her funk as if she'd thrown an inner switch. 'Why don't we work on a suspect list?'

'OK. Sure.'

She raised a declamatory finger. 'I have to stay one step ahead of that boyfriend of yours, now that he knows as much as I do.'

'This isn't a game, Mother,' I chided. 'And, anyway, you're the one who spilled all your info to him. He didn't even have to make an effort.'

'Don't rub it in.' Her eyes grew disturbingly large behind the magnified, over-sized glasses. 'And you *don't* think it's a game to the murderer? A deadly one? To keep from getting caught? Him or her against us?'

She had a point.

In the library, Mother rolled out the ancient school-house blackboard from its spot behind the old upright piano that nobody played, save for a few midnight mice tinkling the ivories.

I took my usual place on its padded bench, Sushi settling by my feet. Meanwhile, Mother planted herself in front of the board, then addressed her classroom of two.

'For the time being,' she said, 'I will dispense with the

London demise of Humphrey Westcott, leaving it in the able hands of MI5, and concentrate instead on the highly suspicious deaths of Ruth Hassler and Tiffany Wallace.'

'Don't waste your chalk,' I said with a wave of the hand. 'It's obvious Jared killed both of them.'

'Is it, dear?'

I shrugged. 'I know you want a complicated mystery to solve brilliantly, and we do have a bunch of players, I grant you. But Jared is it.'

'Oh, now it's a game of tag we're playing, is it?'

I ignored that. 'Jared obviously wanted his mother-in-law's money, so he went over to her house, surreptitiously, and let himself in with Tiffany's key. Then he pushed Ruth down the stairs to make it look like an accident.'

'How exactly did he manage that, dear?'

'Oh, there's lots of ways.' Ducking that, I shifted on the seat, getting into high gear. 'Afterward, when Tiffany began giving him grief about spending so much of the inheritance – or perhaps she'd suspected what he'd done – he got rid of *her*, too.'

'You're long on theory,' Mother said, chin lifted, 'and short on detail . . . but I do agree Jared is our main suspect for both murders.'

Feeling emboldened, I said, 'So that makes Jared the one who broke into our house!'

'Does it, darling?' Mother said, bestowing upon me a small, patient smile, as if dealing with a pupil who'd arrived on the short bus.

She began to pace, like a defense lawyer in a movie in front of a jury. 'Then tell me, dear, just how Jared could have accomplished that? Didn't Tony confirm by way of an impartial witness that the aforementioned Mr Wallace was at the tag sale all day? Right up until being contacted about his wife's unfortunate condition?'

I thought for a moment, though I admit I'd wilted some. 'Then maybe . . . Jared had an accomplice?'

'Are you up-talking, dear? You know how that annoys me.'

'No. I'm asking a question.'

'Good. Because your question suggests that, however much we may suspect Jared in this affair, we *still* have need for a list – but we will set Ruth Hassler's death aside for now, and concentrate only on Tiffany's murder.'

She turned toward the board, picked up white chalk from its lip, and began to write.

When Mother was finished, the board looked like this:

MURDER OF TIFFANY WALLACE

Suspect	Motive	Opportunity
Jared Wallace	inheritance	yes
Skylar James	possible affair	yes
Angela James	jealousy	yes
Colette Dumont	?	yes

I commented, 'So you're limiting the suspects only to people who were at the tag sale.'

Mother nodded. 'Because Tiffany was almost certainly killed by a slow-acting poison administered during that period of time.'

'*Possibly* slow acting,' I corrected, then raised a finger as if testing wind direction (though in the case of a hot wind, it always came from Mother's direction). 'We don't have the autopsy results yet. And what if a *fast*-acting poison had been waiting for Tiffany in that coffin?'

Mother's jaw dropped. 'That hadn't occurred to me. Good thinking, dear!'

Suddenly I'd been promoted to the top of the class! Of course, my only fellow student was Sushi.

'But,' Mother said, 'how would that poison have been administered? Surely not by mouth!'

'Something within the coffin that she might inhale?'

Mother was nodding. 'Possibly. Possibly.'

'Or she took it *herself* by mouth. Something she had with her. The lozenge we postulated.'

Her eyebrows had climbed above her glasses. 'A suicide?'

'A suicide in that case, yes. We don't know enough about

Tiffany and her private life to determine whether she had a motive to take her own life. But we can't rule it out.'

Mother began pacing again. 'Let's explore the notion that the poison, however it was administered, was waiting in that coffin.'

'OK.' I was all for that. I mean, it was my theory.

'Since Tiffany arrived late to the session,' Mother said, 'after the other coffins had already been assigned, by way of participant photos . . . the one coffin remaining, *sans* photo, was obviously reserved for the murder victim.'

'But who would have had access to the coffins before the class?'

Mother thought for a moment. 'Well, naturally, Tilda herself, who set them up in the crematorium room. And, I suppose, any one of the attendees *could* have snuck inside the crematorium before going into the meeting room.'

I raised a 'stop' palm. 'You're forgetting Mr Dunn, who provided the coffins.'

Mother made a face as if smelling spoiled milk. 'Nonsense. Ned Dunn had no motive for dispatching Tiffany.'

'How can you say that? How much do you really know about the man? And Tiffany's life remains largely a mystery.'

Mother put hands on hips. 'Are you trying to be difficult?'

'No,' I replied. 'But what about this scenario: daughter visits mother, there's a heated argument, and *Tiffany* pushes Ruth down the stairs. The police see it as an accident, but Dunn thinks the death looks suspicious. He confronts Tiffany, she offers him a bribe, and, in need of cash for his business, Dunn takes it. Later he regrets having done so – realizing Tiffany has made him an accessory to murder. Then along comes Tilda, asking to use his facility for her "Appreciating Life Through Death" session, and when Dunn realizes Tiffany is attending – maybe even as late as when she walks in the door, presenting the opportunity – he takes advantage of the situation while everyone is in the meeting room.'

'Taking advantage how?' Mother asked.

'Don't you think a funeral director would have something

lying around that could be lethal if injected or inhaled? She might have reclined onto a waiting needle!'

Now Mother was nodding and pacing, pacing and nodding. 'And Ned had a new metal roof put on the building not so long ago, which couldn't have come cheap. But . . . why would he have called Ruth's death to my attention?'

I shrugged. 'Guilt? Casting suspicion away from himself, maybe? Or perhaps once Dunn got involved, Tiffany started blackmailing him, and he thought an investigation by you would put a stop to it, or put her behind bars.'

Mother turned toward the board, and wrote: 'Ned Dunn,' 'blackmail,' and 'yes,' in the columns. She looked back at me with new respect. 'Anyone else?'

'What about Michael Hughes?' I asked. 'He could be the accomplice you posit, which would explain a lie about Jared not ever leaving the tag sale.'

She was shaking her head. 'He's an *old* friend, dear.'

Old friend was code for former paramour.

'Should that,' I asked, 'eliminate him from suspicion?'

'No,' she admitted. 'But I do like the way you used the word "posit."'

'Thank you,' I said. 'After all, Mr Hughes certainly had the opportunity to poison Tiffany's coffee. So you'd better add him, too.'

She put chalk to board.

My focus turned to the second name on Mother's list. 'Do we think Skylar James was having an affair with Tiffany?'

Mother nodded, then reiterated the incident she'd accidentally witnessed – if anything overheard or seen by a snoop like her could be deemed 'accidental.'

'Maybe he *was* just comforting her,' I said.

'First impressions are quite often valid, dear,' she replied. 'And my first impression was that there was something between them, underscored by the way they quickly pulled apart upon seeing me.'

'You mean they acted guilty.'

Mother nodded. 'And the first words spoken by Tiffany – "It's not what it looks like" – told me it was *exactly* what it looked like.'

'I can't really picture Skylar being attracted to her.'

'Perhaps not *her*, dear – but what about all her recently inherited wealth?'

I frowned. 'The economy *has* been pretty hard for antiques dealers. And Angela's teaching salary would only go so far. But why would Skylar murder his, as you'd put it, "paramour"?'

Mother shrugged rather grandly. 'Perhaps she called off the affair.'

'Hmm . . . A little thin as a murder motive.'

She tried again. 'Suppose *he* broke it off, and Tiffany threatened to tell Angela.'

'Or expose something to Angela that Tiffany knew about Skylar! Some criminal activity he was involved in to prop up his business!'

The room fell silent, save for Sushi's light snoring – our conversation apparently struck the little dog as boring after the excitement of all that hammering.

Continuing down the suspect list, I said, 'If the affair *was* real, and Angela felt threatened by it, then it's plausible *she* could have poisoned Tiffany. Maybe not thinking it would kill her – just as a nasty kind of warning.'

'It *is* difficult to get the correct dosage,' Mother said, 'when attempting to not *quite* kill someone.'

I frowned. 'But then – why wouldn't Angela just confront *Jared* about the affair, and let *him* get Tiffany back in line?'

'Perhaps she did, and he tried and failed,' Mother said.

'Which brings us back to square one: Jared.' That left one suspect. 'What is Colette Dumont doing on your list?'

'The rich and renowned Ms Dumont had no reason to attend such a minor tag sale,' Mother said rather grandly, 'unless it was for a *nefarious* purpose.'

Why did I think Mother just liked having someone of that woman's standing as a suspect? Someone she admired, and could justify investigating? Class up the list a little.

I asked, 'Did Colette buy anything?'

'Well . . . yes,' Mother admitted.

'Which *does* justify her being there. What purchase did she make?'

She flipped a hand. 'I don't really know. Jared had already loaded whatever it was in the trunk of her car. But it could have been just a token buy, just as I had done.'

Which brought us to another key question . . . what were we going to do with one Snowbaby?

I asked, 'Anything you might like to add about Colette?'

Mother had a 'tell' – when holding something back, her eyes avoided mine. She got downright shifty.

And finally she said, 'The woman mentioned that she was attending a local auction in the afternoon.'

'So she could have just been killing time at the tag sale,' I said, 'on her way there. *Not* in attendance to kill Tiffany by slow-acting poison. And whether she attended that sale or not is easy enough to confirm.' I paused. 'Did Colette and Tiffany interact?'

'Very little that I witnessed,' Mother said. 'But there could have been more contact before I arrived.'

'What do you see as Colette's motive?' I asked, noting the absence of one.

'To be determined.'

Mother definitely wanted to class up the suspect list.

'Colette also had a conversation with Skylar,' she said, 'which I was unable to hear.'

'We should ask him about it,' I said.

The cozy room fell silent again.

Then Mother lamented, 'If only I had allowed Tiffany to tell me what she wanted to.'

That was the first I'd heard of that. 'When? What?'

'Just before we went into the crematorium. But there wasn't time then, so we agreed to go for coffee later. *Un*-poisoned coffee.'

'Too bad,' I said. 'Might've been important.'

'Indeed.' She returned the chalk to the lip on the board.

I rose from the bench. 'Well, I'm hungry. What are you cooking for dinner?'

Mother's eyebrows rose above the rims. 'Why me?'

'The hammer? You lost the bet.'

'As I recall, I didn't accept your terms.'

'But you *were* wrong,' I pointed out.

She shrugged. 'It's all irrelevant with no verbal agreement or handshake, much less anything in writing.'

I grunted. 'So that's how you're going to play it. OK, then I'll "cook" – how do peanut butter sandwiches sound? Jelly optional.'

Mother grimaced. 'Very well . . . I'll fix Labskaus.'

Yum! That was a recipe passed down from Vivian Borne's Danish grandmother. (And an antidote to Mrs Mulligan's spicy stew.)

She continued, 'Besides, we're going to need a hardy hot meal before venturing out later this evening.'

I should have known. Labskaus usually came with a price.

'Venture where?' I asked.

'To look up Skylar. This entire misadventure began with him. Maybe the answer will start there, too.'

'Maybe even end,' I said.

Labskaus
(Beef and Vegetable Stew)

2 lb. boneless beef
2 lb. potatoes
4–6 carrots
1–2 stalks celery
4 parsnips
1 small head cabbage
2 tbl. minced parsley
black pepper

Cut or chop beef in bite-size pieces. Wash the vegetables; pare the potatoes, scrape the carrots, celery and parsnips, then cut or chop all vegetables into pieces. Place chopped meat in large pot, and add lightly salted water to cover, bring to a boil and cook until meat is tender. Skim the top of fat, and add all vegetables. Use more boiling water if needed, but only enough to cover the vegetables and be absorbed by the time the stew is done. Cover pot with a lid and cook on medium low heat for a little over an hour or until done. Stir in parsley, and black pepper to taste. Makes 8 servings.

A Trash 'n' Treasures Tip

To properly insure your antiques, get them appraised for value, keep an updated inventory, and understand the terms of your policy. Mother refuses to insure any sterling silver, hoping the stuff gets stolen and she doesn't have to polish it anymore.

EIGHT
Carry On Teacher

After dinner, just before seven p.m., Mother, Sushi and I ventured out to the Ford Fusion under dark clouds rolling in from the west, distant thunder threatening to disrupt a peaceful spring evening. Mother Nature was providing us with an unsettling mood.

Behind the wheel, I asked, 'You have directions to Skylar's house?'

'North on River Road,' Mother replied.

I handed Sushi off to her, and started the car.

Long ago I stopped bothering to ask Mother if we should call ahead before dropping in on anyone. Her answer was always pretty much the same: 'What, and give them a chance to make some excuse? Not on your Nellie! Besides, it's the element of surprise that helps me gage reactions to my questions.'

And anyway, to be perfectly honest with you, I get a perverse pleasure out of witnessing the reactions of un-suspecting victims when they open their doors to reveal Vivian Borne standing on their stoop. In Serenity, finding Mother come calling is second only to finding the sheriff on your doorstep . . . and when she *was* sheriff, what a double whammy that was!

Following the winding Mississippi, River Road was a narrow two-lane that sometimes came disturbingly close to the water, which had become choppy as the wind picked up. The moon drifting in and out under the shifting clouds created shadows at once lovely and troubling.

We remained silent, me concentrating on the road, watching for the occasional deer to dart across, Mother mulling over questions to ask Skylar, while Sushi – who normally curled up on Mother's lap – stood facing forward intently, sensing we were out on a mission, the little figurehead at the bow of our hybrid ship.

The intuitiveness of the dog never failed to amaze me. For example, we were nearing the turn-off leading to Tony's cabin home, at which point Sushi would usually begin to quiver and quake in anticipation of seeing Rocky; but tonight she didn't flinch. Why? Maybe because Mother was along. After all, Sushi and I never went to the cabin with her. It was a place of refuge, after all.

Veins of lightning flashed, turning the early purple-pink dusk into sudden inky night, big drops of rain splattering on the windshield like ill-fated bugs.

As we approached what the locals called Colorado Hill, I tightened my grip on the wheel. The stretch of highway was called such because, for one brief mile, you were magically transported from typical flatland Iowa to a winding Colorado mountain road, with rocky bluffs, pine trees, and a majestic view of the river below.

At the top there had long been a lookout, wide enough to accommodate one or two cars. But years of mud slides and erosion had eliminated the spot, so that the only thing between road and cliff was a meager guardrail.

Colorado Hill was beautiful in the winter, spring, summer, and especially the fall – any time of year . . . just not at night. And particularly not in the rain. Or when blinding headlights came at you as you neared the crest.

Like now.

I held my breath, the oncoming car passed safely, and then we were winding back down into the soothing boredom that was Iowa.

At the bottom of the hill, Mother said, 'The next turn.' Which could only be left, unless we were all in the mood for a swim.

For a quarter of a mile, we bumped along a narrow dirt lane guided only by our headlights, then continued up a short incline to the leveling off of a bluff, where several bright security lights popped on, revealing an unusual ranch-style hacienda constructed of burnt-adobe brick with a red-tiled roof.

One concession had been made to the structure, allowing

for the inclement Midwestern weather: an attached garage, shut tight. With no other vehicle in the driveway, we may have made the trip for nothing.

Still, a few lights were on in the house, so I pulled the car into the drive, and we exited hurriedly under Mother's umbrella, me holding Sushi, big raindrops splattering our barely sufficient covering.

A flagstone walk led to two steps up to a wood-carved door, where a pair of potted cacti on either side acted as mute sentries, an overhang providing further protection just as the sky really opened up. The rain was coming at an angle, though, which encouraged us to keep using that shared umbrella as best we could.

Mother's finger was poised at the bell when the door opened as quick, and as startlingly, as another thunderclap, revealing Angela James, wearing a colorful blouse, dark jeans, and a surprised expression.

(While noteworthy in its wide-eyed way, Angela's reaction upon seeing Mother did not knock out my top contender, Mr Fusselman*, who – glass in hand – once did a spit-take worthy, Mother said, of Danny Thomas, a reference that younger readers may wish to Google, if they have nothing better to do with their time.)

'Oh!' Angela said with a hand to her chest. 'I thought you were my husband.'

Vivian Borne had been mistaken for many things, but never a man, with the exception of when she went incognito (*Antiques Wanted*).

Disappointed, Mother said, 'Ah, then Skylar's not home, I take it.'

Angela shook her head, dark tresses bouncing off her shoulders. 'No, he went out just after dinner, right before six.'

'Do you expect him back fairly soon?' she asked hopefully.

'Well, uh . . . yes.'

'Then we'll wait,' Mother replied with cheerful finality.

Angela hesitated, but stepped aside.

I asked, 'Do you mind . . .?'

I was indicating Sushi in my arms.

With only a hint of irritation, Angela again shook her head.

We went in, Mother leaving her umbrella on the stoop. The large entryway was as colorful as a kaleidoscope – high-glossed red-tile floor, vivid wall mosaics, ceiling painted with white moons and blue stars, and a bench decorated with howling coyotes in an artsy fashion.

Also greeting us was the lingering aroma of a Mexican meal, making Sushi's presence moot, as far as sniffing out our home invader.

'Lovely house,' I said, to break the strained silence. But I meant it.

'Thank you,' our hostess replied curtly. 'We wanted to bring New Mexico with us.'

'Oh, it's a lovely state, New Mexico,' I said. 'You must miss it.'

Angela arched a beautifully-shaped dark eyebrow. 'I do.'

Not 'we,' I noted.

She led us into a more subdued main room, which had plaster walls, open wood-beamed ceilings, and a bank of front windows offering a stunning vista of the river in the distance, now glimpsed only during the occasional flash of lightning.

A conical-shaped open fireplace hugged one wall, and the continuation of the red-tiled floor was mostly obscured by a large rug woven in a Native American print. The furniture ran from shades of dark brown to light beige, some pieces rough-hewn, but others, like the couch and an armchair, upholstered in soft leather.

'Would you like something to drink?' Angela asked, perfunctorily. 'Coffee, tea, lemonade?'

'Very gracious of you,' Mother replied. 'But we're fine.'

Me, I would have loved some lemonade. But since Angela was on our suspect list for poisoning Tiffany, I kept my mouth shut.

We sat on the couch, Sushi on my lap, while Angela took a straight-back chair with a cowhide seat to one side of us.

'I understand you're a teacher,' I began, my job being to begin a benign conversation.

Angela wasn't having any of that, responding with a cursory nod and looking at Mother, moving past any small talk with, 'What do you want with Skylar?'

Mother, perhaps thrown a little, shifted on the couch, and said, 'I wondered if he'd heard the sad news about Tiffany Wallace.'

Angela frowned. 'He did mention at dinner that she'd apparently had a heart attack.' Then, out of politeness or perhaps a sense of propriety, she added, 'How is she?'

'Oh, she's dead, dear.'

Angela reared back a little. 'My God . . .'

That reaction seemed genuine enough. If Skylar *had* known Tiffany was dead, he'd apparently failed to share that information with his wife.

Mother, working to sound pleasant and not bluntly interrogative, asked, 'Did you know the woman well?'

'Not really.'

'Ah.' Innocently, she asked, 'And Skylar?'

Not innocently enough, apparently, because Angela's eyes flashed. 'If you're referring to this morning . . . he mentioned to me that you walked in on him consoling Mrs Wallace.'

Mother splayed a hand against her chest. 'My dear, I do not refer, and did not at the time *infer*, that I'd witnessed anything improper. I merely thought that if they were friends, he would want to know of her passing.'

Our hostess appeared appeased. 'I believe Skylar only knows – only *knew* – Mrs Wallace through his business dealings with her mother, Ruth Hassler.'

Mother nodded. 'I see. Then perhaps Ruth had sold him some of her antiques in the past?'

Angela shrugged. 'I'm not sure if they ever came to an agreement on anything – really, I'm not at all involved with the shop. That's Skylar's domain. You'll have to ask him.'

'Thank you, dear. I will.'

The woman's eyes narrowed, and she cocked her head. 'Are you here in some *official* capacity, Mrs Borne? Because this is sounding more like an interrogation than an expression of neighborly concern.'

Mother's little laugh might seem genuine to the untrained

ear, but I knew differently. 'Oh, goodness, no! I'm no longer sheriff. Though I do retain a badge with certain privileges. Even authority.'

That was stretching it.

Meanwhile, Sushi, tiring of my lap, jumped to the floor and settled on the rug. Angela, to her credit, looked at the little dog with a faint smile. She clearly liked Soosh best among her uninvited guests.

Mother continued, 'The thing is, dear, Tiffany did not die from a heart attack.'

Now Angela's attention returned sharply to Mother. 'Oh?'

'The doctor who attended her in the ER feels she may have been poisoned. Of course, the autopsy will tell.'

Angela, looking horrified, sputtered, 'You . . . you can't be *serious* . . .'

'I'm always serious, dear.'

Even regarding the most trivial of things.

Recovering, Angela asked, 'When would this . . . this poisoning have happened?'

That struck me as odd. Not 'why,' or 'where'. . . *when*.

'This morning,' Mother said. 'Quite possibly at the tag sale, although her death occurred some time later. But, as I say, more will be known after the autopsy.'

Mother had got a rise out of Angela the first time she used that unsettling word, and was clearly hoping for a repeat performance.

She was disappointed. Angela merely looked at her watch and said, 'Skylar should have been back by now.'

No longer making any effort to conceal an interviewing-a-suspect approach, Mother went on, 'You were at the sale. Did you notice anything out of the ordinary? Other, of course, than your own presence, after saying you have little to do with your husband's profession.'

Angela stood, said, 'I'm going to call him,' and left the room.

Our reluctant hostess seemed distracted, perhaps really wondering why her husband was so late getting back; but she might have just been ducking Mother's persistent grilling.

I looked at the ex-sheriff. 'Well?'

'She either knows, or suspects, something.'

'I concur. But if you keep pressing like this, she's bound to balk. We'll be back out in the storm toot sweet.'

Mother nodded. 'I do not disagree. She's already skittish.'

Angela was back.

'Skylar's not answering his cell,' she said with what certainly seemed to be real concern.

I asked, 'Does his shop have a landline?'

Angela shook her head. 'He canceled it to save on expenses.' Perhaps regretting any negative reflection cast upon his business, she added, 'Most people know to call his cell phone.'

Mother waved a hand. 'Nothing to worry about. He's probably on his way and didn't answer due to the nasty weather. Keeping his hands on the wheel!'

Underscoring Mother's words, thunder clapped over our heads as rain continued to pelt the windows, as if hundreds of tiny creatures were trying to get in.

'Yes, I'm sure you're right,' Angela said with an uneasy smile, and returned to her chair.

Mother shifted on the couch. 'I must say, I was absolutely thrilled to finally meet the elusive Colette Dumont at the tag sale – what an interesting woman! Had you had the pleasure?'

'No.'

'Perhaps you're unaware of how unusual her attendance was, since you are not "into" antiques. But in all my years in the business, I never caught sight of her out in the *wild* before.'

'Skylar mentioned she's a . . . big deal or something. In your trade.'

Mother forced a laugh. 'I hear she found something to buy at the Hassler manse, and I'm just dying to know what it was.'

Angela's glance conveyed her own wish for Mother to just die. 'I have no idea.'

Mother, regrouping, took another tack. 'I understand you're quite the Agatha Christie afficionado.'

Angela shrugged. 'Somewhat – but I prefer modern mysteries. You two do true crime or something, don't you? I like cozies.' She stood abruptly. 'I'm going to head out and see if Skylar is still at the store – his phone may be dead, and that's why he's not answering.'

In other words, here's your hat, don't let the door hit you you-know-where on the way out.

'Why don't we take you?' Mother suggested solicitously, in a last-ditch effort to continue questioning the woman. 'Then you can return with him.'

When Angela hesitated, I said, 'The road is really slick, so taking one car does make sense. Besides, if you'll forgive me . . . you seem upset.'

'I am,' she admitted, and sighed. She shook her head, her worry obvious. 'It just isn't like Skylar not to let me know he'll be so late. He said he'd only be an hour at most.'

Mother and I got to our feet and followed our hostess into the foyer, Sushi trotting behind.

When Angela opened a closet onto the usual outerwear, Sushi darted inside, then began barking.

Our hostess looked at me quizzically.

'She wants to get home,' I said, and retrieved the little furball. 'She's just loves to burrow in our closets.'

A lie.

Reaching for a raincoat, Angela turned her back to us, and I shared a look with Mother.

Sushi must have reacted to the scent of something – but with both Angela and Skylar's belongings intertwined, whose scent was *it?*

Mother retrieved her umbrella, handing it to me, and I ducked under with her, Sushi in my free arm. Then we made a bold beeline for the car. In the downpour, it was amazing how quickly I got drenched between handing off the umbrella and getting in behind the wheel.

Mother didn't fare much better, having trouble closing her bumbershoot (her term) once she'd reached the front passenger side. We both sat, sopped, waiting for Angela.

Adding insult to injury, Sushi shook the rain from her thick fur, dousing us further.

The back door opened and Angela slid in closing her own umbrella, relatively unscathed.

The drive into town was a nerve-wracking, white-knuckled, lip-biting trip, during which I could barely see the markings on the highway. Even the occasional flashes of lightning didn't help illuminate the road, momentarily blinding me as they did.

No one spoke – not even Mother – with the silence punctuated only by the angry sky's rumbles and bangs and the wipers frantically doing their scraping best to clear the windshield.

I would have pulled over to wait out the storm, had there been anywhere safe to do so; but with the river now on my left, and ditches on the right, the best option was to keep crawling along, hoping any vehicle coming up from behind would notice my tail lights before their slammed-on brakes made it too late.

When we finally reached the safety of Serenity's outskirts and a widening road, a collective sigh of relief filled the Fusion.

Angela said, 'I'm glad I didn't make that drive myself. Thanks for this.'

'Not at all,' Mother said brightly, adding, 'I found it exhilarating!'

Harrowing was more like it.

Angela directed me to go through the alley behind The Trading Post to a place by the store's rear door where Skylar would park his Jeep Cherokee.

But we found the spot empty.

'I don't understand it,' Angela said – it was almost a moan. 'He didn't pass us on the way. I was watching!'

'Try his cell once more,' I said.

She speed-dialed her husband, then said, 'Damn. It went to voice mail again.'

'Why don't we go in?' Mother suggested. 'Perhaps there'll be some indication of where he might've gone.'

This was half trying to be helpful, half an opportunity for her to snoop. Well, make that 40% helpful, 60% a chance to snoop.

Angela was nodding. 'A note to himself on his desk, maybe, or something on his wall calendar. The security system will be on, but I know the code – the last four digits of his cell number.'

I gave Mother a sideways look, which she did not acknowledge; our shop's code was its landline's number, something I had been opposed to.

I pulled into the empty space.

We exited the car, Sushi under an arm, no umbrella now, the torrential rain mercifully having abated to a drizzle. Angela led the way to the back door, where she abruptly faced us.

'I don't have a key,' she lamented. 'I left the house in such a hurry, I didn't even take my bag!'

'May I?' Mother said, with a slow-motion gesture of a graceful hand to herself. She turned languidly toward me. 'Brandy, dear?'

I handed her Sushi, scurried back to the car, dug inside Mother's purse, and returned with what she wanted.

Angela's eyes widened at the sight of the two small lock picks.

'With your permission?' Mother asked, in the manner of a mere formality.

The woman nodded.

In under a minute we were inside, Angela flipping on a light, then entering the code into a wall alarm system and putting a halt to the high-pitched warning tone. We were in a mailing room with stacks of cardboard boxes, packaging material, and a worktable with scale and label printer. Opposite us, an open door led to darkness.

Sushi, annoyed with being passed back and forth, squirmed from Mother's arms and hopped down.

Angela, moving forward, said, 'I'll check the office.'

Mother fell in behind her; but I hung back.

The last time I entered another antique dealer's office, as you'll recall, the outcome was less than wonderful, and I had no desire to go through *that* again. But would it be unkind of me to suggest that Mother likely relished perhaps finding another murder victim?

And the possibility presented itself that Mother and I might make a convenient alibi for Angela, had she killed her philandering husband earlier, after dispatching Tiffany . . .

'Coming, dear?' Mother asked over her shoulder.

'Yup.'

But I'd let them go first.

The layout of the store was the typical Victorian boxcar

style, like the Cinders bar, the second room being an inventory area with shelves for storing antiques, plus a work bench for repairs or other TLC before tagging.

The third room was Skylar's office.

After Angela went in and flicked on the lights, and I didn't hear a scream, I joined them. The space was surprisingly neat – most antiques dealer sanctums I'd been in were a disorganized mess.

This office was divided between living and work areas. One side was mid-century wagon-wheel furniture (chair, two end tables, coffee table) and a brown Naugahyde-covered couch; the other was home to a blond desk and matching file cabinet, with the standard equipment found in any small office, including a closed laptop computer with a few papers neatly stacked to one side.

Western memorabilia covered the pine walls – everything from a collection of silver spurs to signed photographs of famous western movie stars (Tom Mix, Randolph Scott, John Wayne, Clint Eastwood) in their shoot-'em-up personas.

At the moment, Mother was looking at a painting hanging over the couch of a cowboy out on the range being bucked by his horse.

'Is that a Remington?' she asked Angela.

The woman, heading toward the desk, remarked without looking, 'Yes . . . a copy of course.'

'And a very good one,' Mother said. 'Not many people can afford an original.'

I had been watching Sushi closely as she sniffed around the perimeter, and now, suddenly, she picked up her pace. Crossing to the chair behind the desk, where a fringed vest had been draped over its back, she stopped, sniffed, barked, and I swooped in to pick her up.

Angela, sifting through the papers by the laptop, hadn't seemed to notice. But Mother gave me a slight nod. We now knew who had broken into our house.

With a sigh, Angela said, 'There's nothing here. Often he makes notes to himself, but . . . not this time.'

'What about the laptop itself?' I asked.

She shook her head. 'I don't have his password.'

Mother put on a look of concern. 'Perhaps it would be best if we took you home, my dear.'

Her performances in the field are often better than the ones on stage at the Playhouse.

She went on, 'I'm sure your Skylar will be there with a perfectly good explanation.'

Angela muttered to herself, 'Good *ex-cuse* maybe.'

What did that mean?

While Mother and I stepped out into the drizzle, Angela stayed behind to turn out the lights and reset the alarm.

The rain had all but stopped, angry clouds having moved on to share their gloom with other communities, a nearly full moon reclaiming the night sky, providing an ivory shimmer to the puddles.

Back behind the wheel, waiting for Angela's return, with Mother next to me holding Sushi, I asked, 'What do you think "gentleman burglar" Skylar was looking for?'

'The necklace, of course . . . but *why*, I can't fathom.'

I frowned at her. 'Couldn't he have been looking for Westcott's book? The one you *should* have given Skylar?'

She twisted toward me. 'Dear, we've been all over that. That thing is worthless.'

'Maybe there was a code marked in it or something.'

A shake of her head. 'I read every page on the way back from London – there were no such markings, and nothing stuck between pages.' Mother straightened as if she'd received an electric shock. 'Good Lord! I think my copy had a marking on the overleaf.'

'Saying what?'

'Property of SL.'

I groaned. What was worse? That mother had stolen her book from the Serenity Library, or that Skylar knew the one he'd been given wasn't from Westcott.

She was saying, 'It was just a tiny marking. He might not have seen it or known what it meant.'

The car's back door opened, putting an end to our conversation.

I looked at Angela in the visor mirror. 'All set?'

'Yes,' she said glumly.

Compared to our earlier expedition, the return drive along River Road was a walk in the park, the moon guiding our way; still, the pavement was slick enough that care was required – I stayed below the speed limit and even the normally impatient Mother made no complaints. Angela seemed off in a world of her own.

But at the top of Colorado Hill I slammed on the brakes, skidding a little, jolting everyone, fortunate not to have a car directly behind me.

'Brandy! What in the world—' Mother began. Then she drew in a sharp breath.

She, too, had noticed the break in the guard rail, where a vehicle had apparently gone through, the metal bent and twisted outward, as if pried apart by a giant can opener.

Angela, seeing it now, too, choked, 'Oh, no!'

'Could it have been that way before?' Mother asked me.

'If so,' I responded, 'I didn't see it in the downpour.'

With no place to pull over, I got onto what little shoulder there was and put on the emergency flashers. Then I leaned over Mother to fish a flashlight from the glove compartment.

'Everyone stay put,' I ordered.

'No,' Angela said firmly. 'I'm coming.'

'I as well,' Mother chimed in.

So much for my leadership skills.

But I didn't argue. Leaving Sushi behind, we exited the vehicle, then gathered at the edge of the breach, where I aimed the bright beam below.

At first, I didn't see anything but the roiling dark river, still riled from the storm; but when a whitecap crashed against the embankment, then receded momentarily, my light caught the tail end of a vehicle just below the surface near the shore.

Angela gasped, 'That's . . . that's Skylar's license plate!'

She started through the metal gash, but I pulled her back, holding on tight as she struggled and tried to break away.

'You can't go down there,' I said. 'It's just too steep. We have to wait for help.'

Mother had stepped away, cell phone in hand, and was calling the accident in.

'But he could be alive!' Angela wailed.

I shook my head.

'How do you know?' she demanded.

I loosened my grip. 'If this had just happened, there would be tire tracks going down in the mud, and there aren't any, because the rain washed them away.'

'If it happened a while ago,' she said desperately, 'he might have survived the crash! Might have got to the riverbank, and walked away . . .'

'Possible. Which also means he's not down there now, Angela.'

Mother rejoined us. 'The authorities have been notified.'

Already, a faint siren could be heard from a first responder, which turned out to be Tony, who (I later learned) had been on the way to his cabin.

Soon, with lights flashing, the chief pulled his unmarked car up behind ours, and exited.

'Is everyone all right?' he asked.

Mother and I nodded.

'We weren't here when this happened,' I said. 'We just saw the guard rail . . .'

Angela cried, 'My husband could still be down there! He could still be alive!'

I gave Tony the slightest shake of my head.

But Mother said, 'He's not visible on the riverbank, but possibly he staggered into nearby brush or trees.'

'We'll do everything we can,' Tony assured Angela. 'We've set up a detour, and Search and Rescue . . .'

Search and recovery, really.

'. . . will be here soon. Unfortunately, because of the location . . .'

Bottom of a cliff, in choppy water.

'. . . their efforts will be hampered, and anyone inside . . .'

Your dead husband.

'. . . will have to be transported back by boat.'

Not an ambulance. Although one would be waiting at the boat landing. With no need for a siren.

Angela was staring at him, trying to absorb his words.

'Thank you, Tony,' I said.

As he stepped away to speak on his cell, I took Angela gently by the arm, and led her over to the Fusion, where we sequestered in the back, Sushi joining us from the front.

Not knowing what to say to the woman, I sat with her in silence, occasionally interrupted by her sobs.

After what seemed like the longest time, but in reality was probably about five minutes, several beams of light found us, and a boat motor could be heard through the partially cracked window.

'I'm getting out,' Angela announced, and did so.

I also exited, holding Sushi, and we joined Mother by the broken guard rail.

Below, bathed in bright lights, bobbed the bright orange Search and Rescue boat, holding two men. One wore a dark shirt, slacks, and life jacket; the other, a diving suit equipped with oxygen, along with a utility belt no doubt containing tools for breaking a vehicle's glass window and cutting off safety belts.

Tony stood several yards away from us, cell in hand, in communication with the uniformed man, who was looking up at him.

Then something unexpected and, frankly, touching happened. Angela slipped her hand in mine, gave it a little squeeze, and I squeezed back.

What transpired next came quick.

The diver went into the water and returned to the surface with Skylar; the driver's partner helped ease the limp, lifeless body into the boat. The motor roared, and the craft sped away toward town.

The fact that the victim had not immediately been given CPR labeled this a recovery. Which Angela understood, releasing my hand, hers going to cover her mouth.

Tony, who'd stayed on his cell throughout the process, ended the communication, then came over to Angela.

Before he could speak, she said, 'I want to be with my husband.'

'It would be best if you went home,' he said gently.

'No.'

Tony nodded. 'I understand. I'll take you to the hospital.'

He escorted her to his vehicle, settled her in the front, then came back to face Mother and me.

The day had been long and tiring and full of surprises . . . but nothing could have prepared me for what Tony told us.

'That was no skid on wet pavement,' he said. 'And the vehicle's back end wasn't hit . . . but the driver's side was.'

Somebody had forced Skylar James off the road, and through that railing.

A Trash 'n' Treasures Tip

Fine-art prints are considered original works of art, and not to be confused with reproductions or copies, which are mass-produced by machine. Prints are created on a copper plate or stone or other medium, then printed in a limited batch, numbered, and usually signed by the artist (if alive) and can be found in some of the world's greatest museums. Mother feels great pride, by the way, in having a Keane 'big-eyed child' print signed by Margaret, not the artist's con-man husband Walter.

NINE
Carry On Cleo

D ear little Brandy had selected 'Carry On Matron' as the title of this chapter of mine, but the editor granted me kind permission to change it. Why? Firstly, I do not consider myself to be a matron! I neither run a British boarding school nor do I behave in the manner of a stodgy old lady, thank you very much. (Did your mind immediately repeat that phrase, 'Thank you very much,' and take you to that rousing number in the stage and film musical, *Scrooge*? If not, it should have!)

Secondly, our more loyal, longtime readers will no doubt recall my connection to Cleopatra, the Queen of the Nile. A few years ago, while under hypnosis administered by Tilda in pursuit of a detail important to a case (*Antiques Chop*), out popped Iras, Cleo's hand-maiden – *moi* in a former life – who was the Queen's asp handler. (Contrary to what history has written, my maidenly hand did not follow the Queen's into that lethal basket; my loyalty to my Egyptian mistress did not extend to such sacrifice.)

The morning following the death of Skylar James by staged auto accident, I went out at eight into the cool spring morning to my waiting Vespa (Brandy and Sushi were still slumbering, angels unaware).

I had a day of investigation planned and was happy knowing my daughter would be working at the shop, out of harm's way (and my hair). Frankly, I had arrived at the conclusion that the higher the body count, the less helpful Brandy is. Murder seems to create anxiety in the young woman.

Anywho, my first stop was the police station downtown, a modern one-story red-brick structure next door to the new state-of-the-art, three-story county jail (the construction of which I had actively campaigned for, after spending an uncomfortable night in its ancient, crumbling predecessor some years ago).

Kitty-corner from the jail (so much more colorful a way to express it than 'cater-cornered,' and anyway, who doesn't like kitties?) stood a magnificent edifice of limestone built in the late 1800s – our courthouse, which looked like a gigantic white wedding cake with a bell tower on top rather than the traditional bride and groom (or groom and groom, or bride and bride, although of course any nuptial couple would have looked ridiculous atop a courthouse, even though any number of such ceremonies were conducted annually within).

The proximity of the two facilities was a master stroke: a criminal could be charged at the police station, escorted across the street for arraignment at the courthouse, then jaywalked to the county jail (certain laws are really more guidelines, it would seem).

I parked my ride in the side lot of the police station, then walked around to the front through a scenic little brick plaza with several stone benches and small shade trees.

The small lobby of the station provided visitors with four uncomfortable mismatched chairs along one wall, an irritatingly humming soda machine in a corner, and a neglected banana tree plant leaning toward a single window as if trying to escape its pot – the depressing decor seemingly designed to encourage short visits by the citizenry.

I marched up to the Plexiglas window behind which a young woman in civilian attire worked diligently at a computer, neglecting her role as receptionist in favor of managerial duties or some such.

Formerly this had been where a uniformed dispatcher sat, but last year – keeping an off-the-cuff campaign promise made during a speech I'd given when running for sheriff – I'd installed a new command center on the basement level that served the sheriff, police and fire departments.

As a civilian, I now regretted that move, as my ex-sheriff 'perks' did not include access to said command center. No good deed goes unpunished!

Gone were the days when I could saunter up to the Plexiglas, engage the dispatcher in conversation with the intent of gaining inside information, discover her weakness, then exploit it by way of an autographed photo of a movie or pop star (which, frankly, I had signed in proxy), a part in my next play (walk-on), or a big box of Godiva chocolates (the contents replaced by those of a Whitman sampler).

'Vivian Borne to see Chief Cassato,' I told the woman, whose name plate identified her as Ashley*.

(*Note to the reader from Brandy*: Don't forget, an asterisk indicates you need not remember this person!)

Without taking her eyes off the screen, the middle-aged woman replied, 'Go on through – he's expecting you.'

Her announcement nearly rocked me back on my heels, and that is more than just an expression to a woman with hammer toes. Usually, Tony keeps me waiting, allowing me time to get out my cuticle scissors and give the leaves of the banana tree (no bananas so far!) a little much-needed pruning.

But, seasoned thespian that I am, I did not divulge my surprise, replying only with a crisp, 'Thank you.'

Ashley buzzed me through a steel door into the inner sanctum and I proceeded down a boring beige-tiled corridor with tan painted walls, the tedium of which was broken by group photos of policemen of bygone days whose eyes seemed to follow me with suspicion, much like those of the living in the local law and order game.

I passed two 'interview' rooms, two detective offices, and one bathroom, whose symbol over recent years I'd seen evolve from a man, to a man and a woman, to a man and a woman plus a half-man/half-woman. Progress isn't always pretty.

Tony's office was on the left at the end of the hall, across from the lunchroom – a position no doubt allowing him to keep tabs on anyone lingering past their allotted time. Suspicion came with his job, apparently.

Upon entering, I found the chief – typically outfitted in a light blue shirt and navy tie (and I assumed pants) – on his multi-line phone in listening mode. He gestured toward the chair opposite him at his desk.

He didn't frown as he did so. How I had rated such a warm welcome, I could only wonder.

Tony Cassato's office, which I'd been in many times before,

was as utilitarian as they come, providing few clues as to the man himself: no mementoes, no award plaques, no photos (not even of Brandy). In fact, Tony had retained the same decor as the man he'd replaced, from the carpet to furniture, including duck prints on a wall arranged as if to fly out the window, perhaps in pursuit of a fleeing banana tree plant.

(Initially at least, Tony had a good reason to keep such a low profile – for those not-in-the-know, the answers are waiting in *Antiques Knock-off*.)

The chief grunted and hung up.

'I was told you were expecting me,' I said.

He leaned back, folding his arms. 'Why? Weren't you planning on showing up anyway?'

'I was indeed. And I am flattered that you deemed to take me into your confidence last night.'

A deeper grunt suggested I shouldn't be. 'Let's get on with it, Vivian – I have a busy day ahead.'

As did I. As did I . . .

'The preliminary autopsy?' I asked.

'Drowning.'

'Any visible injuries?'

'To the head. Consistent with hitting the steering wheel.'

'Could the damage to the driver's side of the jeep have been caused by an oncoming car crossing the center line?'

'No. The scraping was back to front.'

'Then, it's your opinion that someone came up behind Skylar, and – while passing – propelled him through the guard rail.'

He chose his words carefully. 'A viable theory.'

'Anything found?' I asked, then qualified the question. 'Cell phone, perhaps?'

A nod. 'Damaged.'

I ventured, 'Some information might be salvageable. Call records could be obtained.'

'Which all takes time. And I'm not sure we have it.'

He rolled back on his chair, stood, crossed to the bullet-proof window (one change he'd had installed himself – again, *Antiques Knock-off*), and looked through the partially closed blinds.

'You think there will be more killings?' I asked.

He half-turned, his expression unreadable. 'Do you?'

I nodded. 'Something is coming unraveled like a sweater caught on a nail. Something or someone.'

He sighed, then came over slowly but steadily. 'I can't quite believe I'm saying this, but . . . I could use your help.'

How I'd longed to hear those words! And how surprised I was that he hadn't choked on them! Had I been more confident about solving these murders, I'd have taken the time to gloat.

'Unfortunately,' I admitted, 'I'm as baffled as you. Absolutely stymied. But I have a few avenues to pursue, and will keep you in the loop.'

When I felt it necessary.

His eyes widened a bit. 'You'll keep *me* in the loop.'

'Absolutely,' I said, ignoring what might have been a hint of sarcasm in his tone.

I stood and was making for the door when Tony said sharply to my back, 'Vivian!'

I turned.

His expression had moved from impassive to grave. 'Be careful, for once. Whoever's responsible is desperate – two murders within twelve hours. You've dealt with bad people before, but this feels . . . different.' He drew in a breath. Exhaled, then added, 'I'd appreciate it if you'd keep Brandy out of it.'

'I'll do my best,' I said, 'but you know that girl has a mind of her own.'

He smiled just a little. 'Don't know where she gets it from,' he said.

Outside the station, I was pondering my next move, when my cell phone trilled – the caller I.D. announced Tilda.

'Hello, dear,' I said, assuming she wanted to discuss yesterday's disastrous New Age death session, and working not to sound impatient.

'You simply must come right away, Vivian.'

Not pleased that my precious time would be wasted on mere commiseration, I asked, 'Might we talk later?'

'It's about Tiffany – something you should see.'

That piqued my interest!

Into my shell-like ear she was saying, 'Can you make it before ten? I have my Pranayama Breathing class then.'

I didn't know what that was and, of course, had no intention of asking. I just said, 'Be there in a flash.'

Or at least as flashingly fast as my scooter would scoot. (Bless you, MasterClass!)

Tilda lived across from Greenwood Cemetery in a white two-story clapboard house, which demonstrated what was once considered dilapidated but might now be seen as shabby chic.

The guru was waiting for me on the porch, dressed in her usual flowing hippie fashion, the Age of Aquarius gone gypsy.

'Come with me,' she said, as soon as I'd ascended the slightly slanting wooden steps.

I followed her inside, where we stood in a large room serving multi-purposes: a shop selling candles and crystals, a waiting area for students, and living space for herself and her many cats. The latter were, typically, roaming about. Each had shown up at her front door over the years – doing so (coincidentally?) shortly after a graveside service had occurred across the way.

Tilda, however, believed the felines to be reincarnations of the recently departed, taking the creatures in and calling each by the name of the freshly interred.

I knew of only one cat, Rufus Dowling*, who wouldn't stay under Tilda's protective roof, and was eventually run over while crossing the street to get back to the cemetery. Now, I happened to know that the human carnation of Mr Dowling had *hated* cats, and I think he may have committed Furry Kiri to get himself a different body. But I don't think it worked because, according to Tilda, a new cat appeared within the hour. (Ironically, Mr Dowling himself, the person I mean, had also been killed crossing the street.)

Her expression clearly troubled, the guru asked, 'Vivian, do you remember those wills we made out at the session yesterday?'

'Certainly. A nice touch I thought.'

'Thank you. But as I was about to throw them away, I happened to look at Tiffany's. Well, not "*happened* to look" – she had actually died, so—'

'Dear, cut to the chase. Remember your imminent Pranayama Breathing class.' Whatever that was.

She nodded, withdrew a folded paper from a pocket of her voluminous skirt, and handed it to me (the paper, not her skirt).

The note read: *The funds in the money market in my name at the First National Bank are not to go to my husband, Jared Wallace, but the beneficiary designated on that account.*

Signed, *Tiffany Wallace.*

'I thought you might find that of interest,' Tilda said, 'since, knowing you, you'll be conducting an investigation.'

'I'm in the process now,' I confirmed. 'Might I keep this, dear?'

'Certainly, if it's any help.' She shrugged. 'Of course, it's not legal.'

'Of course it isn't.'

But I was less sure of that than I sounded, though knew of someone who could confirm or deny my suspicion of what this document might portend.

Wayne Ekhardt had been my lawyer since Brandy was in diapers. Now a near centenarian, Wayne still retained a few clients, myself included, and kept only limited office hours a few mornings a week. Occasionally, he would still appear in court to defend a client, not often enough these days for judges to learn never to ask him to approach the bench, and initiate an interminably long trip to and from.

As a young man fresh out of law school, Wayne had made a name for himself in the Midwest by obtaining a Not Guilty verdict for a woman who had 'accidently' killed her philandering, abusive husband by shooting him in the back several times. (Like-minded Serenity husbands took note of the outcome, and curbed their hedonistic ways, for a time, anyway.)

Wayne had his office in the Laurel Building, an eight-floor Art Deco edifice he had once owned, running a thriving law practice on all but the main floor, which had been a department store, and the top floor, which he rented out to various professionals.

But after five decades, the attorney sold the building to an engineering firm, under the stipulation that he could retain the uppermost floor, rent-free, for life – a sweetheart deal that, considering how long the codger has hung on, has soured with his hosts with each passing year.

I entered the remodeled but still retro glass-and-chrome lobby, took an elevator up, then stepped off into a world that had not changed since the 1940s. While the engineering firm had promptly gutted all the other floors, keeping up with modern times, Wayne hadn't changed a thing in his domain, retaining the old scuffed black-and-white speckled ceramic-tiled flooring, scarred-wood office doors with ancient pebbled glass, Art Moderne sconce wall lighting, and even an old porcelain drinking fountain. Any letters put through the ornate brass mail slot on the wall next to the elevator would most certainly not be delivered.

Wayne's office was at the end of the hallway, facing the river, and as I walked along, passing vacant offices, I could almost hear the sounds of a lost era coming from behind locked doors: the grinding of a dentist's dull drill, the yelp of a child receiving a doctor's shot, the hard-sell pitch of an insurance man to a client, the clacking of a receptionist's Royal typewriter.

I'd always wanted to get behind those locked doors, to see what treasures had been left behind; for now it would have to remain on my bucket list.

At Wayne's office, I rapped on the pebbled-glass door, receiving no answer – perhaps this time I *should* have called ahead. I tried the knob, which squeaked like a mouse in the throes of torture, then stepped inside.

The legendary defender was seated behind his grand old desk, his nearly bald, liver-spotted head tilted back, his eyes closed, mouth open, like a bird waiting for a worm from its mama. He appeared even more fragile than usual in a suit that had become too large. More than once I'd been greeted by such a sight, which always gave me a start, as my first impression was invariably that my old friend and fellow justice warrior had finally passed into the care of a celestial magistrate.

And this time I would have bet an artificial hip that Wayne had received a final verdict.

I moved gingerly toward him, and – having neither a feather

nor mirror to place under his nose, nor easy access to the gnarled hands beneath his desk to check for a pulse – I gave his shoulder a little poke to see if he'd fall over.

But to my great surprise his rheumy eyes fluttered open, and he struggled to focus on his guest.

Ah! I still had representation!

Wayne tried to speak. Coughed. Coughed some more. Then he managed to croak, 'Vivian, what a pleasure to see you!'

'And you,' I said, meaning it.

At one time, a considerable number of years ago, after our respective spouses had passed away, I could have snagged this brilliant man, who always seemed interested in me as more than just a client. But a successful defense attorney's wife can too often find herself feeling incompetent, irrelevant, and immaterial.

'Please, Vivian, sit, sit,' Wayne said, gesturing with a bony hand to the client chair opposite.

I did so.

Then, pulling his shrunken self up into his suit, in a hopeless effort to fill it, he asked, 'What brings you around on this fine spring day? Something interesting, I hope. I could use a little excitement.'

'Excitement,' I said in jest, 'is the last thing a man your age needs.'

He laughed, which led to another coughing jag. When it abated, he managed, 'Not me, Vivian! I'm still firing on all cylinders.'

If running out of gas. And how many cylinders did a Model T have, anyway?

'What's on your mind, young lady?'

I risked initiating another coughing fit. 'You do realize that's a dangerous question?'

He smiled this time, his teeth still his, and original issue. 'Do I have to tell you that we retain attorney/client confidentiality?'

From my purse I produced Tiffany's handwritten will, then pushed it across the massive desk.

Wayne picked the paper up and, while studying it, remarked, 'This is the woman who had a heart attack in the casket.'

Even at nearly one hundred, Wayne kept up on local events.

'Yes,' I said. 'Only, it's suspected to be murder.'

He looked at me with a new sparkle coming to the old eyes. 'Is that so? Interesting. Interesting.'

I began to explain, perhaps in too much detail, because toward the wrap-up, Wayne leaned back in his chair, sank into his suit, and closed his eyes.

I'd lost the old boy!

Or so I'd thought, until – after I'd finished – the eyes popped wide. I jumped a little. It was a bit like Boris Karloff suddenly opening his eyes in *The Mummy*.

He said, in a cool, clear voice worthy of a courtroom, 'And you want to know if this written note is legal?'

'Yes.'

'It is.'

I sat forward, countering, 'But Tiffany's signature wasn't witnessed.'

'Wasn't it?' he asked with an impish smile. 'Weren't there others present who saw her write the will, and could sign affidavits to that effect?'

By golly, he was right!

'You could argue that in court?' I asked.

'With confidence. If it comes to that, just let me know, and I'll rush to your side.'

Trying not to picture that, I said, 'Thank you, Wayne.'

'Any time, young lady.' He handed me back the paper.

'And,' I said, rising, 'send me a bill for your services.'

'When I get around to it,' he said.

Which the dear man has rarely ever done.

My next stop was the First National Bank, one of downtown Serenity's few modern buildings, a red-brick-and-glass three-story structure that sprawled along the riverfront.

In the spacious lobby, I approached the reception area and informed the young woman that Vivian Borne would like to see Gladys Gooch, who had recently become my new personal banker.

The receptionist swiveled away from me, spoke briefly on

a phone, then said Ms Gooch would be with me in a few minutes, and would I please take a seat in the waiting area.

I went over to a sectioned-off space that contained padded office chairs, side tables with magazines, and a coffee station. Above a wall fireplace (not lighted this time of year) was a small flat-screen tuned to a business channel with captions fighting a crawl that displayed stock prices of a not-so-robust Wall Street.

I had barely settled into a chair when Gladys appeared, a plump, pleasantly plain woman in her mid-thirties, with mousy brown hair I'd never been able to get her to do anything about, wearing a conservative navy blazer with skirt and sensible pumps.

I'd met Gladys last fall when she was employed as a manager of a small branch office in a nearby town. At the time, I was sheriff, working on perhaps my most difficult case (*Antiques Ravin'*), and the woman provided me valuable information in exchange for a promised part in a play – a lead role, no less. Since then, Gladys had relocated to Serenity and become active in our community theater.

(Sidebar: good-hearted Gladys proved to be a simply dreadful actress – quite the hopeless amateur who had never trod the boards, even in school. Out of desperation, to save my reputation as a director, I'd taken Gladys to see Tilda, whose under-hypnosis suggestions made the amateur's opening night performance a sensual thing to behold! Unfortunately, the suggestions began to wear off after a few days – sometimes during the play itself – so I had to keep Tilda backstage, like a sports team's doctor, ready to apply mesmeric first aid.)

Gladys, her big brown eyes shining like Sushi's when I dangled a doggie treat, said, 'Oh, I hope this is about the new play!'

I rose and met her eyes. 'It is indeed. I have just the role for you.'

She clasped her hands together – goody-goody! If only her talent matched her ambition.

When Gladys continued that childish posture, I asked, 'Might we go back to your office, dear?'

'Oh, certainly!'

As we walked along, passing identical cubicles, I engaged in small talk – how was she? How did she like her new job at the bank? Wasn't the weather beautiful? Anything to avoid specifics about a new thespian challenge for the girl. This I did all the way to our destination.

Gladys claimed her spot behind the L-shaped metal desk, and I took one of two chairs facing her.

'Have you decided upon one?' she asked eagerly.

'One what, dear?'

'What *play* you're going to direct next. What my *role* will be!'

'Oh.' I shifted in my seat. 'I am strongly considering *The Brothers Karamazov*.' Which I of course had no real intention of staging, as – even with the Vivian Borne touch – it would go over in Serenity like a lead balloon.

Confused disappointment clouded the shiny eyes. 'I'm going to play a man?'

'Oh, no, dear. Grushenka.'

'Gesundheit.'

'I wasn't sneezing, dear. That was a name.'

'Is it a good part?'

My little smile teased and promised. 'Marilyn *Monroe* seemed to think so.'

'She *did*?'

I leaned back, tented my fingers. 'It was Marilyn's dream to play Grushenka – one unfortunately never fulfilled before her untimely death.'

'Tell me about this . . . Grushilda.'

I didn't bother to correct her. 'Well, dear, the character is young, beautiful, proud, fiery, headstrong, sexually alluring. Right up your alley.'

Glady's eyes sparkled like dull diamonds. 'Oh, my! Do you think I'm up to it?'

'No actor is better suited for the part than you,' I lied.

The woman sat back, giddy with the news, patting her hands like Eddie Cantor (unintentionally, since the *Whoopee!* man was well before her time, and maybe yours).

I leaned forward. 'And now, dear, first things first – I must get down to business.'

Which brought Gladys out of her euphoria.

'Business?' she asked, blinking.

Hadn't the girl learned yet there was always a price to pay? Even for the promise of a part in a play that would never happen?

'Yes,' I replied. 'I need to know if Tiffany Wallace had a money market account with the bank, in her name alone, and if so, the amount and the beneficiary.'

Gladys frowned. 'Oh, I don't know about that, Vivian. You aren't sheriff anymore.'

'I'm an *Honorary* Sheriff, dear, with all the rights and privileges that go with the title.'

Which she wouldn't know amounted to very little.

'Would you like to see my badge, dear?'

'No, no. That won't be necessary.'

'Good. Now . . . the information?'

Gladys turned to her computer, the keyboard clicking under her flying fingers. In seconds, she said, 'There is a money market account in Tiffany Wallace's name.'

'And the amount?'

'Two hundred and fifty thousand.'

'And the beneficiary?'

'Michael Hughes.'

Well, dear reader, you could have knocked me over with a feather – I had been expecting Skylar James! Apparently, Michael had 'tagged' Tiffany for more than a percentage of the tag sale.

'Thank you, dear,' I said, masking my surprise, as if the information she shared had zero import. 'I'll let you know when I finalize the decision about the play.'

I stood.

Gladys looked up at me. 'Would it be helpful if I told you that Tiffany had changed the beneficiary from her husband to Mr Hughes . . . just a few days ago?'

Helpful indeed!

'Good to know,' I said off-handedly. Then I smiled, said, 'You will make a simply *wonderful* Grushenka,' and left.

Perhaps yours truly should have felt at least a tiny amount of shame for misleading the young actress regarding the play

– but who's to say I *wouldn't* produce *The Brothers Karamazov*? The wheels were turning. I could cut it from five acts to three – add some original music. Russian dancing. Hey!

Besides, this was no time for self-recrimination; I had a killer to catch.

By around noon, feeling hungry, I decided to grab a bite. Rather than go to a busy bistro, where I would run into chatty acquaintances, I needed somewhere quiet to think.

At this hour of the day, not a soul was in Cinders except Renny, who was up on a ladder behind the bar removing a string of lights that had lost their twinkle. I knew the feeling!

Wearing a purple cold-shoulder top, pink crinoline skirt, and black leggings, the hostess had heard the door open, and twisted her head toward me.

'Hello, Vivian,' she said warmly. 'I'll be done in a minute.'

'No hurry.'

The menu at Cinders was limited to frozen pizza, frozen chicken tenders, and frozen pork sliders. Well, they weren't frozen after the microwaving. But Renny usually also had soup she would bring from home.

'What's the special today?' I asked, nodding toward the crockpot behind the counter. 'A delicious aroma is wafting!'

Renny descended the ladder, saying, 'Chili con carne.'

'Sold – *con brio!*' Renny's notoriously spicy homemade concoction might mean certain aftereffects would be left in my wake, but that would be Brandy's problem.

I filled a red-bucket chair at the center of the bar.

'Anything to drink?' the proprietor asked, facing me.

Since the air conditioner was going full blast, I replied, 'A hot toddy. But hold the toddy.' Which was pretty much hot water, honey and lemon juice.

While Renny was preparing my repast, I asked, 'How are Nona and Zelda getting along?'

Ladling a generous serving of chili into a Styrofoam bowl, she responded, 'Fine, fine. Only . . .'

Renny placed the bowl in front of me, along with a plastic spoon, a few crackers and a napkin.

'Only . . .?' I prompted.

She leaned forward conspiratorially, the left half of her generous bosom nearly dunking itself in the soup. 'Zelda's been coming in here by herself.'

Worried that Renny had lost her marbles, I kept my expression neutral. 'You don't say.'

She nodded. 'As a matter of fact, Zelda's here right now. I think she followed you in.' Renny's eyes went to the end of the bar. 'She's right down there.'

Well, what did I have to lose? I swiveled in that direction. 'Zelda, would you like to join me?' Then to Renny I said, 'Some chili for Zelda.'

Before Renny could react, the front door opened and Nona came in, the Goth-dressed young woman exclaiming, 'Oh, *there* you are!'

I thought Nona was looking at me, but she strode to the adjacent chair, and addressed it.

'One moment we're waiting for a table at Salvatore's,' Nona said with exasperation, 'and the next you're gone!'

Silence.

Nona nodded. 'Oh.' She glanced at me, then back at Zelda. 'Well, what did you want to tell her?'

Longer silence.

Nona looked at me. 'It's about that man who had that accident last night.'

'Skylar James,' I said.

Nona nodded. 'Zelda says that when we left here yesterday evening, she saw him talking to a woman.'

'When? Where?'

Nona consulted Zelda.

'About six-thirty, in his store across the street,' Nona said. 'He was closed, but the lights were on, and when we went by, Zelda noticed them through the front window.'

I asked the empty chair. 'What did this woman look like?'

Again I waited for Nona to relay the response.

'Zelda only saw her from behind,' the woman said. 'She had dark hair. And they seemed to be arguing.'

That could be Angela! Had she suspected Skylar of having an affair with Tiffany, who she poisoned, then hours later dispatched her cheating husband after an argument? Had the wronged wife already played Ben-Hur chariot race with her husband before *we'd come calling last night, giving her the opportunity to play concerned and distraught for us?*

If so, where did Michael Hughes fit in?

I began to address Nona, but then remembered to query Zelda herself: 'Can you tell me anything else about what you saw?'

A moment.

'Not really,' Nona said, then turned quickly to the empty chair, listened, and added, 'but there was a fancy car parked in front of The Trading Post.'

'What kind of fancy car, Nona? I mean, Zelda?'

Another moment.

Nona said, 'A silver one.'

I knew someone who drove a silver Jaguar, and so do you, if you've been paying attention.

Lovely, dark-haired Colette Dumont.

Vivian's Trash 'n' Treasures Tip

Money can be made in the buying and selling of antique office equipment, such as old calculating machines and typewriters, fountain pens, electric fans, wood file cabinets, and swivel chairs. Brandy bought an ancient, cracked-leather couch out of a psychiatrist's office – I think she meant it as a joke (in very bad taste, I might add), but claimed she intended it as a place for me to collect my thoughts. I tried that, but always seem to fall asleep on it, which is not surprising, as I have often fallen asleep in psychiatrists' offices.

TEN
Carry On Cruising

Welcome back – Brandy speaking.

Foot traffic at the shop had been steady throughout the morning, easing up nearing noon, so I was enjoying my lunch break, seated at the boomerang-infested Formica table in the kitchen, having a cold turkey sandwich from home.

The bell above the front door jingled, signaling my repast was past, but before I could even rise, Mother came rushing into the kitchen.

Looking frazzled, she announced, 'I need you to take me somewhere!'

'Can't you take yourself on your Vespa?' I asked, adding, 'It's not raining or anything.'

She ignored both my question and statement. 'Somewhere out of town. Right now!'

My eyes narrowed. 'Where?'

She hovered. 'Iowa City. I have an appointment with Michael Hughes, and he'll only be available for another hour and a half.'

That was a forty-minute drive at least.

Mother barreled on, 'And then I'll want to speak to Colette. We'll have to take Sushi – no time to drop her off home. No time to call your friend Joe to take the helm here.' She turned toward the front and pointed, a sailor seeing an island on the horizon. 'I'll retrieve the flags. Chop-chop!'

Didn't she mean, 'Land ahoy'?

I growled, but Sushi didn't, waiting patiently at my feet for the last bite of my sandwich and getting more than she'd hoped for, to her delight.

Soon all three of us were piling into the Fusion.

Knowing some time could be shaved off the trip by

eschewing Interstate 80 for secondary roads, I headed west out of town, rather than north.

Along this more scenic route, Mother filled me in on the rather astonishing array of things she'd learned this morning: Tony confirming Skylar's jeep had been forced off the road; Tilda revealing Tiffany's impromptu will mentioned a money market account left to someone other than her husband; our ancient but astute lawyer claiming said will was valid; Gladys identifying Michael Hughes as the beneficiary of that surprisingly substantial account; and Zelda seeing a woman who was almost certainly Colette Dumont arguing with Skylar at The Trading Post shortly before the man's murder.

'You *have* been a busy girl,' I remarked, genuinely impressed. 'I assume you're meeting with Michael to try to learn what's behind this money market account Tiffany attached his name to.'

'That and more, my dear. That and more.'

She had other thoughts to share and I took them all in.

Thirty minutes later, cruising through a lush Grant Wood-esque landscape, we were nearing the outskirts of Iowa City when Mother instructed me to turn off onto an asphalt road at the top of a hill. This I did with a squeal of the hybrid's tires, as this guidance came typically last second.

Soon I was pulling into the gravel drive at an idyllic-looking farmhouse setting: white picket fence, white two-story with latticework, welcoming wide porch, red barn with wrought-iron rooster, and even a windmill, its silver blades turning lazily in the breeze.

Yet it was clear this was not a working farm. No crops were to be seen in the fallow fields, no cows, pigs, or chickens – free-ranged or fenced – and not even so much as a small vegetable garden. It would seem the fastidious Mr Hughes wanted all of the romantic bucolic trappings sans the back-breaking work that might put any troublesome dirt under his manicured fingernails.

The middle-aged man with neatly trimmed beard, wire-framed glasses and studiously casual attire – button-down shirt with rolled sleeves, dark jeans, and slip-on shoes with tassels and no socks – was waiting for us on the open porch.

We exited the Fusion and, since there would be no containing Sushi in these temptingly verdant surroundings, I allowed her to roam free, though she was neither cow nor chicken.

Hughes, his demeanor pleasant, descended the few wooden steps. 'Why don't we talk on the porch, ladies,' he said. 'I've made lemonade.'

Just right for this pastoral setting.

We followed him.

Among a grouping of wicker furniture including a table with a waiting tray of three glasses and sweating pitcher, we took two of the four chairs while our host settled into one opposite us.

Michael filled the glasses with the sweet and tart concoction; but neither Mother nor I partook of any of the drink until he'd had his first.

Few smiles were more forced than hers when she asked, 'Where were you last night, Michael?'

Smile or not, it was a verbal slap and his trimmed eyebrows rose. 'Here. Why?'

'Can anyone verify that?'

Hughes frowned, and he again said, 'Why?'

Mother's frown conveyed only curiosity. 'You *have* heard that Skylar James is dead?'

His glass, headed to his lips, halted, sloshing a little. 'Why no, I hadn't. What on earth happened?'

'Briefly, he wasn't on earth at all. His jeep went through a guard rail on Colorado Hill during the deluge last night.'

He seemed to be over the shocking news already. 'How unfortunate. The rain was bad here, too.'

Mother took a dainty sip of her glass. 'Oh, the storm wasn't the cause.'

'Is that right?'

She nodded sagely. 'According to Chief Cassato, someone *deliberately* forced Skylar off that cliff and into the river.'

Oddly, that got only a faint smile out of our host, who set his glass down. 'All right, Vivian . . . I know you well enough to realize this is not a social call.'

'Indeed it's not.'

His grunt was not quite a laugh. Flatly he stated, 'You suspect I had something to do with it.'

Mother arched an eyebrow. 'I suspect you may have. I make no accusation.'

'Glad to hear it.'

'But did you?'

Hughes stared at her, as if perhaps she were an illusion that might fade. When she didn't, he said, 'Vivian, please. I barely knew the man. Why in God's name would I do such a terrible thing?' He sighed irritatedly and picked his glass back up, and took a defiant drink.

'Perhaps because,' she said, her tone triumphant, 'both you *and* Skylar had been having affairs with Tiffany.'

He made a face like the lemonade was too sour. Seemingly unimpressed by her charge, he said, 'That's ludicrous, Vivian.'

'In which case,' Mother said, rolling right along, 'you would also have killed Tiffany.'

Hughes looked at me. 'Is your mother out of her mind?'

'Figuratively or literally?' I asked. It was always a question worth debating, if one had the time.

He went on, quietly indignant, 'I understood Tiffany had a fatal heart attack.'

'No, dear. That was merely the preliminary diagnosis. The autopsy concluded she was poisoned.'

Mother was bluffing – the report wasn't in yet.

She went on, 'With suicide unlikely, it seems probable her coffee had been doctored in a deadly manner during the tag sale. The poison was a slow-acting one, you see.'

He said nothing. His face might have been stone but for an occasional blink.

Staring him down, Mother continued, 'You had ample time to slip something into Tiffany's coffee . . . you may recall the cup she'd been drinking from – it had a kitten on it.'

Hughes scoffed, 'So that means I killed Tiffany . . . why? Because I was jealous, due to this imaginary affair? Or did the bad taste demonstrated by that kitten cup drive *me* momentarily mad? A good thing I had some slow-acting poison along!'

Mother smiled sweetly. 'No, neither jealousy nor an issue of taste was at the root of this evil – *money* was.'

This time his grunt was definitely a laugh. '*What* money?'

She gave him a patronizing look. 'You expect me to believe you knew nothing about Tiffany making you the beneficiary of a money market account leaving you a quarter of a million dollars?'

Hughes appeared stunned, all the blood leaving his face. 'Wh-what . . .?'

'You heard me, sir.'

'No, no, I *didn't* know! If that's even *true*.'

'Oh, it's true all right.'

I entered the fray. 'In which case, why would Tiffany pointedly exclude her husband and make you the beneficiary, if you *weren't* involved with her?'

He drew in a breath, as if about to respond. But he didn't. For endless seconds, he just stared with even the blinking stopped.

We waited.

Finally, he spoke. His voice was soft now, nothing defensive in it, nothing at all indignant.

'All right,' he said, 'I did have an affair with Tiffany . . . briefly. But even calling it an affair is a gross overstatement.'

'What was it then?' Mother asked.

His shrug was loose and kind of pitiful. 'I don't know *what* you'd call it. It just kind of happened when she came here to finalize the contract for the tag sale. She was an attractive young woman and I've been alone for . . . it's been almost five years since I lost my wife.'

I hadn't known he was a widower. Mother surely did.

'But,' he was saying, shaking his head, 'I didn't know *anything* about the money . . . you must believe me.' He paused. 'She . . . she was miserable in her marriage, and I think, well, coming here, to this lovely farm of mine, she could imagine herself living with me. I thought at first she saw me as a father figure, but . . . it was more than that, different than that. Only . . .'

I finished his sentence. 'You didn't feel the same way about her.'

He lowered his head, and nodded. 'It came about so fast that I didn't think beyond the excitement of . . . of a fling with a younger woman.'

Mother said, 'So when you told her the affair was off, she
threatened to make trouble for you, ruining your reputation,
and your business.'

Frowning, with some of the indignation returning, Hughes
sat forward. 'It wasn't like that at all! I hadn't even gotten
around to telling her.' He sighed. 'And then, when I heard she'd
died . . . well . . .' His tone was melancholy now. '. . . I didn't
have to tell her, did I? It was too late to tell her anything.'

Mother's voice took on an atypical edge. 'After you *silenced*
her, you mean.'

He looked at her in earnest. 'Vivian! You *know* me. Do you
really think I'm capable of killing *anyone*, let alone two people
I barely knew?'

Mother studied him. Really studied him. Then, dejectedly,
she shook her head and uttered, 'No. Not really.'

He sat back, let out a deep, relieved sigh.

Mother, apparently suddenly realizing the folly of placing
a double murder at this man's feet, said, 'Besides, if you *had*
known about the money – and poisoned Tiffany for it – why
would you bother running Skylar off the road?'

'I would think,' he said, sounding hurt, 'that you realize
this horrible thing you've suggested is nothing I would be
capable of doing . . . over some, some . . . petty affair.'

Still, there was nothing 'petty' about the quarter of a million
smackers Tiffany had left him.

Mother, regrouping, asked, 'Did your "younger woman"
ever share any confidence with you, other than random snip-
pets about her unhappy marriage?'

Our host frowned. 'Funny you should ask that – I *did* get
the feeling something else might be troubling her. But, if so,
she never quite got around to expressing it.'

*Was this the 'something' Tiffany had wanted to talk to
Mother about?*

Hughes was saying, 'Anyway, if Skylar had been having an
affair with *anyone*, it would've been Colette Dumont.'

Mother, eyes flashing, pounced. 'What makes you say that?'

The man seemed to regret his words. Then he shook his
head. 'I wouldn't want to put anybody in the position you've
put me in.'

'Michael,' she persisted, '*someone* is killing people in our little antiquing circle. If you know anything, you need to say.'

Finally Hughes shrugged. 'Well . . . Skylar and Colette had been doing some business together.'

'What kind of business?'

'I don't know, exactly.'

Or at least he wouldn't say, no matter how much Mother tried to shame or scare him. That was obvious.

So she took a different tact. 'Do you know if Colette bought anything at the tag sale?'

His eyes tightened in thought. 'No . . . I don't believe she did – oh . . . wait. She *did* make a purchase, at that. I only noticed, and then kind of forgot about it because – well, it was such an inconsequential item for her to pick up.'

'What was it?'

'A box of books.'

Mother frowned. 'Valuable?'

A dry laugh. 'Good Lord, no. That's what made it inconsequential. I nearly didn't include them in the sale.'

'What were they?'

He thought a moment. 'Old Agatha Christie mysteries. Cheap reprints.'

'Anything in particular?' Mother persisted. 'Poirot titles? Miss Marple? Standalones?'

'Good lord, Vivian, I don't know!' he said, showing some irritation. 'I didn't write up the sales ticket – my assistant did.'

Mother smiled, as if that might heal the wounds of this contentious conversation. 'Might I possibly see that sales ticket?'

'It's on my computer,' he replied, as if that were enough to deter her.

Foolish man.

'A copy will do,' Mother replied sweetly.

An exasperated sigh came up from his toes and seemed to propel him to his feet. 'Very well . . . but only if you will promise to then go. I told you when you called that I have an appointment to keep.'

'And miles to go before you sleep?' Mother asked. 'That's just a poetical rhetorical question, dear. No need to reply.'

He looked at her for a while, as if trying to decide whether or not to strangle her, then decided against it and entered the house, the old farmhouse screen door slamming behind him, as if it were as put upon as he was.

I opened my mouth to say something, but Mother held up a hand. Whether she wanted silence for contemplation, or perhaps thought Hughes might be listening, wasn't clear. Either or both were possible.

Several minutes passed before our beleaguered host returned to present Mother with a print-out, like Simon Legree delivering an eviction notice.

She studied the page, then passed it to me.

Recorded as sold to Colette Dumont were the early novels of Poirot, beginning with *The Mysterious Affair at Styles* and ending with *Hercule Poirot's Christmas*.

Murder on the Orient Express, which should have been included, was not on the list. That title was certainly starting to turn up. Was that significant? And why was an upscale dealer like Colette interested in Christie reprints at all? Just a fan, maybe?

Hughes asked Mother acidly, 'Happy?'

She looked up at him. 'Ecstatic.'

'Thrilled to hear it. I simply have to leave – you've already made me late.'

If he was expecting an apology from her, it would not be forthcoming.

Sardonically, with a mock gracious gesture, he added, 'But, please, *do* sit and finish your drinks.'

'Thank you,' I replied, when Mother said nothing.

Hughes walked to the barn, where he opened the double doors, then disappeared within.

Shortly after, an engine started, then a white van backed out, straightened, and drove away, leaving a trail of dust.

Neither side of the vehicle was dented.

One of the reasons we were here was to see if the dealer's vehicle bore signs of having 'helped' Skylar over the side of Colorado Hill.

After taking the last sips of our lemonade, we left the porch and were heading for the Fusion when I realized I hadn't seen

Sushi for a while. My eyes made a trip around the lush grounds looking for her, but she was nowhere in sight. I had a moment of dog-owner panic . . .

. . . but then *there* she was, trotting out of the barn.

Hughes had exited in such a huff and a hurry, those wide doors had been left open wide, and our furry little sneak had slipped in for a look around.

Mother raised an eyebrow. 'Sushi had a quick peek around – why shouldn't we?'

'Because your dear old friend Michael might come back.'

'Well then, my child, we were merely closing up the barn so no one would get in, weren't we?'

Inside the barn, instead of finding farm implements lining the walls, or livestock in stalls, or hay in the loft, the structure revealed itself as having been gutted for storage. Around the periphery, on deep metal shelving, were hundreds of boxes; the central area was reserved for the now-absent van with plenty of room for loading and unloading.

I walked over to the nearest shelf where a carton was labeled HASSLER in black marker.

Behind me, Mother said, 'What didn't sell at Ruth's tag sale, he'll donate to a good cause.'

'I always wondered what happened to the leftover stuff at tag sales.'

'Yes, and in this case the good cause is solving two murders. Go ahead, dear.'

I untucked the top flaps on the box.

Mother peered over my shoulder. 'What's in it?'

I sifted through the contents. 'Seems to all be greeting cards – *decades'* worth.'

Mother made a shivering sound. 'I *know* people like that – save every single one they get!'

She retained a card for only the day of celebration, then into the trash it went, no matter the sentiment. I have a hunch some people, receiving her Christmas letter in the mail, didn't wait that long.

'Here's one in a frame,' I said, holding up a fancy gold card behind glass with printed words, 'Happy 50th Anniversary To My Loving Wife.'

'Take it out, dear,' Mother said. 'There's bound to be an inscription for that Golden moment.'

I slid the back off the frame, and handed her the card.

Mother opened it and read aloud: 'You've always dreamed of having a signed first edition of your favorite Poirot. Perhaps next year I can find you the cover. Love, Harry.'

Our expressions mirrored each other – stunned, bug-eyed, mouths open darn near as wide as the barn doors.

Her words came in a rush: 'What the devil happened to that book from the Old Curiosity Shop I was supposed to give Skylar?'

Mine came just as fast: 'I added it to the ones we bought from Dumpster Dan, to take to the recycle station!'

She clasped her hands in prayer. 'Please tell me you didn't take them!'

'I didn't.'

She nodded to the sky, then beamed at me. 'I can always count on you to not follow through.'

'Thank you very much.'

She sang, 'That's the nicest thing that anyone's ever done for *moi!* . . . Where's the box?'

'In the trunk.'

Back at the Fusion, Mother once more examined the book she had brought back from London.

Her sigh was one of frustration. 'So much for that hunch. It's a *reprint*. And not the original first edition cover.'

'Are you sure?' I asked.

She handed me the book, and brought out her phone.

Soon, Mother put the screen under my nose. '*This* is the first cover, published in 1934 by Collins Crime Club in the UK.'

The illustration depicted two men in silhouette stoking coal into a fiery train engine.

Mother tapped the one in my hand, with its image of a train in snowy landscape. '*That* is the reprint by Crime Club in 1953.'

I grunted, and was about to toss the book back into the box when, on impulse, I removed its jacket and the plastic sleeve . . .

. . . which revealed a second cover beneath!

One with the original coal-stoking depiction.

Mother gasped. 'A cover within a cover! How clever.'

'We had it all along,' I marveled. '*That's* what Skylar was looking for when he broke into our house!'

She nodded, eyes big – *really* big, behind those thick lenses. 'And paired with Ruth's signed golden anniversary present, the book would now be worth a hefty sum.'

'Where do we go from here?' I asked.

'Well, dear, we're already in Iowa City – perhaps we should do some shopping . . .'

Mother used her cell. In a moment I heard a feminine voice, with just a hint of French accent, saying, 'Antiques Fantastique.'

'Ah . . . Colette Dumont herself!' Mother chirped. 'How wonderful! Vivian Borne speaking. I'm in town with my daughter, Brandy, who I know would love to meet you, and see your incredible shop.'

'I'll be here until closing, Vivian,' the woman said, business-like but friendly. 'You're welcome to stop by.'

'Will do,' Mother told the cell. '*Au revoir!*' She ended the call.

We looked at each other.

'She knows it's a ploy,' I said.

'And I *know* that she *knows* it's a ploy,' Mother said.

'And *she* knows that *you* know that *she* knows it's a ploy,' I added.

'And that's all we need to know,' Mother said.

Antiques Fantastique was located in the downtown midst of Iowa City – home to the University of Iowa – just far enough away from student bars, second-hand stores, and inexpensive eateries to maintain an air of exclusive respectability.

Parking on the street in college towns is always fraught with peril, what with the lack of spaces, limited time on meters, and outrageous cost of fines. So I immediately punted (Go, Hawks!), heading to the closest public garage – a four-tiered monstrosity – which happened to be just across the street from Colette's establishment.

After I'd gotten my ticket and the mechanical arm of the barrier gate had raised in its jerky, put-upon way, Mother said, 'Go to the left.'

'Those are leased spots,' I protested.

'Exactly.'

'She wouldn't risk parking her dented car here.'

Mother shrugged. 'She might have. Who from Serenity would ever see the thing?'

'Nosy would-be amateur sleuths?'

'Just do it, dear.'

We cruised the leased area, going up and down each row, looking for a silver Jaguar, but finding none. No shortage of hybrids like ours, though.

Several empty reserved spots indicated one *could* be leased by Colette, who had perhaps thought better of driving a car involved in a vehicular homicide.

After parking on the upper level, and cracking the windows for Sushi, Mother and I made our way down the echoey stairway, then jaywalked across the street to a modern concrete building. A sign on the glass entrance of Antiques Fantastique recommended clients make an appointment. But the door was unlocked.

I don't know what I'd been expecting, but the ultra-modern, sparse interior might best be characterized as more a gallery than an antiques shop, its white walls displaying oil paintings in heavy gilded frames with sculptures and other *objets d'art* balanced on Greek pedestals.

Oh, there *were* antiques, mostly Louis the Fourteenth (or Fifteenth?) furniture and Tiffany lamps and other high-ticket items. But nothing actually *had* a ticket – if you have to ask, *mon cheri*, you can't afford it.

We were met by an attractive – make that *stunning* – woman perhaps in her forties (or possibly fifties, with the help of a very skilled *artiste de scalpel*) with sleek, dark medium-length hair and perfectly understated make-up. She looked *très chic* in her gray tweed Chanel suit and designer heels.

The wide red mouth spoke. 'How nice of you ladies to drop by.'

Introductions were made, and Colette offered me her hand,

which was at least as cold as her violet eyes, all of which went with the chill temperature she maintained in the shop.

Mother began, 'You're lucky to have that parking ramp just across the way. Places on the street are scarcer than hen's teeth.'

Fortunately, Mother was in detective mode and all of us are spared a discussion of whether hens actually had teeth and, if so, what were they like, exactly.

'Yes,' the woman said with a wisp of a smile. 'That ramp is the reason I chose this location. It certainly wasn't the architecture of this building.'

Mother's laugh sounded phony, but then it always kind of did. 'I suppose leasing a parking spot across the way would be sky-high.'

'I wouldn't know,' she said with a tossed-off smile. 'I walk from home.'

'How invigorating!' Mother's eyes went to the woman's feet and those designer shoes – five (hundred) will get you ten (thousand) the soles were red. 'But surely not in *those*, dear.'

Colette's laugh seemed just as phony as Mother's. 'Of course not – not in *Louboutins*.'

Do I know my shoes?

'Please have a look around,' she said, pleasantly dismissive, 'and do let me know if I can be of any help.'

If the woman had hoped to extract herself with that, Mother put an end to such a foolish notion.

'Oh, you *can* be of help,' Mother replied.

'Oh? Is there something here you're interested in?'

'Yes. Answers to a few questions. Now, I understand you spent some time last night with Skylar James at The Trading Post. Am I correctly informed?'

'You are,' Colette replied, folding her arms; then she made a sad face. 'Such a tragedy – I heard about the accident from his wife.'

Mother's eyebrows went up. 'Really? From Angela?'

Colette nodded. 'She gave me the terrible news when I phoned to talk to Skylar this morning.' She waved a red-nailed hand. 'It was regarding an item in her late husband's store that I'd inquired about. We couldn't come to an agreement as to price last night, so I was going to try again.'

'What was the item?' Mother asked.

Colette hesitated. 'I'm sure you'll understand that I wouldn't want the information to get around, as I'm still hoping to acquire it through his wife.'

Mother splayed a hand upon her bosom. 'My dear, as one dealer to another, you may consider me the soul of discretion.'

As opposed to the sole of Louboutins.

The red mouth twitched in mild irritation. 'Very well . . . it was a painting.'

'Ah . . . the Remington oil,' Mother said.

Colette's surprise was obvious. 'That's right. Perhaps you've noticed it in Skylar's office.'

'I have. But Angela claimed it was merely a copy.'

Colette's smile was knife-edge thin, a red cut thanks to the lipstick. 'Well . . . Skylar may have *told* her that, so she wouldn't know how much he'd paid for it.'

'I see.' Mother filed that away, then asked, 'Did Skylar say *why* he was willing to part with the painting? For a man with a collecting interest so focused on the Old West, a Remington must have been quite the rare prize.'

A shrug. 'Isn't it obvious? In this financial climate? We're *all* having difficulties, from the bottom . . .' She nodded toward us, then lifted her chin. '. . . to the top.'

Gotta hand it to her – Colette did know how to lob a snobbish insult.

'The reason I'm inquiring, dear,' Mother said, 'is that it appeared to a passerby that you and he were engaged in an argument.'

Colette's smile grew strained. 'Please. You know how it can be between dealers. How it can look more heated than it is, haggling. Just some friendly bartering, that's all.' Yet another shrug. 'As I mentioned, we couldn't come to a meeting of minds.'

'What time did you leave The Trading Post?'

She thought for a moment. 'Between six thirty and seven . . . exactly when, I can't say. It had started to rain, and I wanted to get back to Iowa City before the storm really hit.'

Mother switched gears. 'Tell me – why did you buy that box of Agatha Christie reprint books at the tag sale? They're common, worthless . . . and you are neither.'

Colette gave a little *c'est la vie* gesture of a delicate hand. 'Tag sales so often are the aftermath of tragedies. It seemed purchasing something, anything, was the polite thing to do, the decent thing. Don't you agree?'

Yes – that's how canny dealers like us can get stuck with a Snowbaby.

Colette, not waiting for Mother's answer, continued, 'The box of books is in the alley dumpster, Mrs Borne. You're welcome to dive in after it, if you like.' The high heels were turning. 'Now, if you don't mind . . . and frankly, even if you do . . . I have business to attend to.'

We watched her disappear into another room of the gallery.

Then Mother – probably aware we were on security surveillance – said, too loudly, 'Isn't she a lovely creature!'

'Uh-huh.'

'Well, we should be going . . . we have other errands to run.'

'. . . OK.'

Adding my part to our exit-stage-right buffoonery, I helped myself to one of Colette's cards on the way out, as if to tell her (or her cameras) that the Borne girls could afford to do business with her.

It wasn't until we were seated in the Fusion, with a pouting neglected Sushi on her lap, that Mother spoke.

'We've *got* to find her car,' she lamented. 'It's the one thing that will tie Colette to Skylar's murder.'

'There can't be many Jaguar dealers around Iowa City,' I said, 'that could do that kind of repair.'

'True enough,' Mother said. 'But I don't think Colette's had time to take it anywhere.' A pause, then: 'Brandy, dear, you know very well that car is stowed in the garage of her house.'

'Please don't say it.'

'Yes, dear, we're going to have to perform just the teensiest, weeniest break-in.'

After which we could be heading for the cutesiest, woostiest jail cell . . .

A Trash 'n' Treasures Tip

Country antiques and farm implements continue to draw buying interest. As the world gets more and more complicated, folks tend to look back nostalgically at simpler times – although our ancestors might take issue with that characterization after cooking on a wood stove, hand-washing clothes, and planting a field with a plow. Mother once bought a butter churn with the intention of using it, but her first attempt at churning threw her back out, and the thing ended up in our shop. Anyone out there want an old butter churn?

ELEVEN
Carry On Spying

C olette Dumont lived in the historic, affluent enclave of Iowa City known as Park Bluffs, about a mile from Antiques Fantastique, making her claim of always walking to work plausible – even if it still didn't ring true to me.

From North Dubuque Street, I steered the Fusion up a sharp incline carved into a limestone bluff overlooking City Park. At the top were seven houses – mansions, really – sharing the scenic ridge, spaced out nicely among tall pines, broad oaks, and drooping willow trees, each exhibiting a different architectural style.

One residence in particular stood out.

'Whoa,' I said, peering through the windshield, half-impressed, half-horrified. 'It looks like a gigantic mausoleum.'

'Indeed,' Mother said. 'But it's a dwelling for the living, all right, if atypical for Iowa City . . . or anywhere else, actually.'

She shifted into know-it-all tour guide mode.

'It was built in 1890 by a protégé of Frank Lloyd Wright, an associate who had worked on the construction of Hollyhock House while the great man himself labored away in Tokyo, building the Imperial Hotel.' A pause, a gesture. 'After the two men had a falling out, the protégé struck out on his own, and *this* humble abode was his first conception.'

I was familiar with Wright's designs, and Hollyhock House in Los Angeles was one of my favorites. Colette's poured concrete edifice displayed many of the same symmetrical stylings – a two-story centerpiece with slanted walls recalling the Mayan Revival period, supported by one-story wings on either side. Yet this structure was somehow even more austere, with none of the whimsical delights of Hollyhock House.

'Does it have a name?' I asked.

This kind of place usually did.

Mother confirmed my opinion: 'Foxglove.'

I could see the design of the tubular flowers etched into the leaded glass of the long narrow windows, the identical motif rimming the edges of the flat roofs. Nearby was a garden of its namesake tall blue plants.

I frowned. 'Isn't foxglove poisonous? Like, *very* poisonous?'

'Yes, dear. Known to cause heart attack and death.'

The implications of that required no discussion, not even from the chatty likes of Mother.

'What now?' I asked.

She gestured regally ahead, as if I were a rickshaw driver and she a wealthy tourist in Hong Kong. 'Drive on, of course.'

Of course.

The road made an oval loop around the group of mansions, until – on the back half of Foxglove – a driveway slanted down through the yard into a lower level that hadn't been visible from the front.

'There's the garage,' Mother said. 'That's where we'll find our Jaguar. Pull over.'

I selected a spot among a sheltering of pines and shut off the engine.

'We really should call Tony,' I said. The time had come for Brandy Borne to be the voice of reason. 'If we're correct in our assumptions . . .' Again, largely unspoken. '. . . the woman in that mansion is a murderer twice over. Why put ourselves at risk, when Tony can easily get a warrant through the county sheriff?'

'Can he, dear?' Mother asked. 'Based on what evidence would he be able to do that?' The coolness in her voice was unsettling. 'All we have are suppositions.' She twisted toward me. 'Do *you* believe Colette is our killer?'

'"Believe" doesn't cover it. Have you ever seen colder eyes?'

Her expression grew wistful. 'I was more struck by their stunning violet hue, rivaling Liz Taylor in Technicolor. Colette Dumont really is a lovely woman.'

I smirked at her. 'So was Lucretia Borgia. Mother, if we're

right, this is obviously a very dangerous person we're talking about.'

Her shrug could not have been more matter of fact. 'Then *we* must act before *she* does . . . because, dear girl, otherwise? *We* are likely to be her next victims. Best take the upper hand.' She leaned toward me. 'If we find the Jaguar, dents and all, we can call your boyfriend and report what we saw. *We* don't need a warrant!'

She was right, though that would likely still land us in the clink.

'All right,' I said with a sigh. 'But we've probably already been picked up by security cameras.'

'Perhaps, but if so, I doubt the woman has any staff monitoring them. This is a residence, not a hotel.'

Again, I couldn't disagree with her. 'What about the sophisticated alarm system she's bound to have?'

'Sophisticated it may be,' Mother said, with a dismissive smirk, 'but *not* one with motion detection.'

Her confidence was maddening.

'How do you know that?'

'There's a cat in the window.' She was handing me Sushi. 'Dear, you have to stay alert in these situations.'

'I would rather stay *out* of these situations.'

'It's a little late to be deciding that!' she said, as if this were all my fault. My idea.

I moaned. 'But what if we get caught?'

Which seemed likely to me.

'If so, assuming Colette doesn't dispatch us in her own home, what would happen then? She would call the police on us, wouldn't she?'

'Probably.'

'And how is that a bad thing, dear?'

Was she kidding? And what about how she skated over that 'dispatched' part?

'Mother, we'd be incarcerated, and I am not at all interested in helping you stage amateur theatrics in stir.'

Her chin lifted. 'I would never impose my will upon you in that way, dear.'

Right.

'But the thing is,' she said with an impish smile, as if we were planning a prank, 'we'd be safer in jail. Wouldn't we?'

Infuriating! But how could I argue with it?

Opening the rider's side door, she said, 'Come along, child. I've already spotted a way to get in. And bring Sushi. Her way with cats like Tilda's may prove a plus!'

We walked down the driveway. Our home invasion was happening in broad daylight, but then many home invasions do, and these mansions were separated from each other by trees and shrubbery, so we were unlikely to be spotted by neighbors.

As we approached the basement-level garage, my first thought was to find windows to look through, which if they revealed the dented Jaguar would make a trip inside unnecessary. But there were no basement windows at all. Even so, holding Sushi tight, I assumed the way in that Mother had in mind would involve going through the garage somehow.

But instead she cut across the immaculately maintained back yard and led the way to the mansion's opposite wing.

Mother brought our little trio to a stop at a cast-iron rectangle embedded in the concrete side, about a foot from the ground. She was gesturing to it in a '*Voilà!*' fashion.

'Seriously?' I asked. 'We're going in through a coal shoot?'

'It's more an aperture, dear. With no more than a six-foot drop. Easy-peasy! I'm up for going first. Then I can pull you through from below.'

I took offense. 'Why? I'm not any larger than you!' Of course, my feet hadn't touched the bathroom scale in a while, and what was I *doing*, anyway, arguing to be able to go first?

Mother knelt, her knees popping like tiny firecrackers. 'These things usually don't have a lock, but let's see if it's wired.'

Carefully, she slid her fingers beneath and along the hatch's rim.

'Doesn't seem to be,' she pronounced with a smile, then slowly opened it.

And something unexpected happened.

Sushi jumped through, and disappeared from view.

Well, at least Mother and I could stop discussing who should go in first.

'Now see what you've done,' I said, aghast. 'We'll *have* to go in.'

Her smile mingled affection and pity. 'Was there ever any doubt, dear?'

'Yes!' Some. A little. OK – none whatsoever.

With Mother hovering, I knelt at the opening and stuck my head through.

Sushi was about six feet below in the basement, eyes shining up at me as if expecting praise, panting, tail wagging, looking unfazed by the drop.

'I'm just going to get her,' I informed Mother, 'and come right back out. This entire enterprise is half-baked, and I'm calling a halt to it!'

'Fine, dear. I will respect that. We're a team, after all.'

Entering the opening feet first, I got stuck at the hips – it actually would have been better having Mother down there to pull me through – but I, well, forced the issue and then dropped to the floor, landing like a cat. A very clumsy cat.

A concrete stairway led up to a doorless entry onto the main floor that provided plenty of illumination.

This was a cement room that had once contained coal, the shadow of which remained on the floor, though the black chunks of fuel themselves were a distant memory.

I was in an aisle, one of several, between stacks of wooden crates of all sizes – the kind for transporting fragile items. This was actually a relief, as I could make my own stack of a number of these, to make my escape easier.

Turning to call up to Mother, I was startled by her head having already emerged from the aperture, her hands reaching out – at least she was having the same problem I'd had with my hips – giving me no alternative other than to pull her on through. It made for a difficult breech birth, particularly the delivery in which she fell on top of me and we collapsed in a pile, with me on the bottom.

Sprawled on the cement floor together, I snapped at her, 'I could've explained *my* action . . . Officer, I was just going after my dog! But *two* of us looks downright criminal.'

Sushi was regarding us curiously, though she'd perked at the word 'dog.'

Mother sat up, dusting herself off. 'Well, the damage is done, and as long as we're here, why not make the best of it?'

I said nothing, as I saw no 'best' in any of this. And strangling her would have looked even more downright criminal.

'Come, dear,' she said, motioning me along. 'Let's keep our eye on the prize!'

'If you mean the presumably dented Jaguar,' I said, tagging after, 'there doesn't seem to be any way to get to the garage in the other wing without going through the house itself.'

Mother saw the wisdom of that – using the term 'wisdom' loosely.

She said, 'Keeping with the symmetrical set-up of this place, there should be another set of stairs in the opposite wing leading down to the garage. What do you say, dear? Shall we explore?'

I didn't bother answering. I didn't even bother sighing. The most irritating thing about all this was what a good time she was having.

With Mother in the lead, and Sushi following and me definitely bringing up the reluctant rear, we ascended the concrete stairs that opened directly into the main living area.

'Well, isn't this a disappointment,' Mother said, looking around in disparaging appraisal.

I, too, was surprised. The vast room was practically empty, but for a couch, floor lamp, and end table grouped in front of a cement fireplace. It was as if Colette had sold off the Steinway grand, Chippendale furniture, and assorted oil paintings, save for one over the mantle – a portrait of a stern-looking man in a pin-striped suit, who I assumed to be the woman's father. The old boy was looking down at the sad surroundings as if sharing our disapproval.

Mother approached the end table, and gave it The White Glove Test, minus any white glove. Looking at her dirty finger, she said, 'I would swear no one's been in here for years. How is that possible?'

I groaned, flashing back to an earlier case in which Mother

had gotten the address wrong, then left behind a ridiculous note saying, 'Sorry! We meant to break into a different house,' along with cash for the smashed window.

This time around, reading my mind, she was quick to assure me no such error had been made.

'This *is* the right place, dear. And Colette Dumont certainly *does* live here – I have that from a reliable source.'

I took that with a carload of salt. After all, some of Mother's sources were highly questionable – need I mention the invisible woman on the Cinders bar stool?

She was saying, 'It's a big mansion – Colette probably only uses part of it.' Casting a keen eye around, Mother went on, 'Besides, *someone* is feeding the cat.'

A sleek black-and-white Siamese had appeared to join our merry break-in band, obviously desperate enough for attention to put up with a strange dog, while Sushi was clearly happy to get to know our feline host.

Now a two-person train with a feline-and-canine caboose, we moved along a wide hallway toward the other wing, passing a large entryway with marble floor and wainscoted walls where a central round table held an elaborate oriental vase. Next came the dining room dominated by an Arts-and-Crafts mahogany table bearing a fine patina of dust, followed by a non-upgraded but modern-looking (in a 1930s sense) kitchen with signs of use, including food on the counter and dishes by the sink. Finally we arrived at a study or, more properly, the library.

This, it would seem, was where Colette deemed to spend most of her time, at least as far as this floor was concerned – we had not gone upstairs to the sleeping quarters. Though every bit as ample as the living area, the library gave the illusion of coziness, thanks to its low ceiling, rich mahogany-paneled walls with built-in bookcases, and poured-cement gas fireplace with a flat-screen TV above it and, facing it, a brown leather armchair with footstool, both with a lot of mileage on them. The decor was again of the Arts-and-Crafts period – Stickley furniture, brass-and-glass table lamps, an oriental rug added for warmth.

To our right, another doorless portal led onto concrete stairs down to the lower level (presumably the garage), mirroring the opposite wing.

I was heading that way, but Mother walked over to a library table with a single book, minus a dust jacket. Positioned with its spine facing a set of tall narrow windows, the book would have been visible from the outside, had we gone window-peeking.

'Is that what I think it is?' I asked.

'Yes, dear,' she said, examining the indicia page. 'Ruth's golden anniversary present, waiting for its rare, expensive cover. It would seem it's been left in this spot to encourage our entry.' She gave me a coolly unconcerned look. 'I would say we may have walked into a trap.'

'Is that our cue to leave?'

'Have we come this far for naught?'

I took a breath and made for those stairs and hurried down, determined to find a Jaguar, dented or not, before we made a hasty retreat.

As I entered the windowless garage, motion lights clicked on in the concrete cubicle, and the news was not good – no Jaguar. But recent oil spots on the cement indicated this had almost certainly been its usual home.

Mother joined me; hugging her feet were both Sushi and the cat, looking up at me.

'So the Jaguar was just *bound* to be here,' I said to her petulantly. 'Any other big ideas?'

'One does leap to mind, yes,' she said, excitement dancing in her magnified eyes. She pointed to a metal door. 'I'll wager that leads to the area between here and the coal room.'

I flapped my arms like a flamingo wishing it could fly. 'We don't have time for any more nonsense! And, please, no more risks! We've *got* to get *out* of here.'

I would swear both the cat and dog nodded.

Calming myself, I pointed toward the door. 'Besides, whatever's behind there rates a security pad. Just how do you propose we get past *that*?'

She confirmed that information with a glance, then asked, 'Where's that card I saw you take?'

'What card?'

'The one you helped yourself to back at Antiques Fantastique – Colette's *business* card, dear.'

I fished it out of a pocket.

Mother took the thing, gave it a glance, walked over to pad by the door, and entered four digits.

The little red light turned green.

'Apparently mine isn't the only great mind,' Mother said, 'to use a phone number for a security code.'

'No comment,' I commented.

As we passed through the metal door, more motion lights were activated, illuminating in an under-lit fashion an elongated room that seemed to stretch on forever – a 'forever' that ran the length of the central house linking the two wings.

We froze after taking a single step into the chamber, agape at a gallery that made Colette's downtown Iowa City establishment seem like the mere facade that it was.

Riches of art were everywhere – on the walls, on pedestals, in glass cases, as if we had entered the tomb of a later-day King Tut Ankh Amun. Besides a similar chill, there was nothing cold about these surroundings, nothing that recalled the concrete walls of the gallery at Antiques Fantastique or, for that matter, the upstairs.

No, here we found a continuation of the mahogany paneling seen in the library, with another brown leather armchair and ottoman in the center of this odd, wonderful, yet somehow creepy space.

'Are these things all for sale, you think?' I asked, wondering if this was where Colette kept her most prized inventory, or perhaps brought her wealthiest clients for private showings.

Mother was taking it all in. 'Possibly, dear. But I don't believe that's the primary function. Note the benches.'

She was referring to the rectangular cement blocks placed strategically apart where one could sit and admire the art and artifacts.

'Then,' I said, 'just what *is* this?'

'Not merely Colette's private stock,' Mother said, 'rather . . . her *collection*.'

As we walked slowly along, gazing at the paintings, I recognized the familiar styles of Van Gogh, Monet, Degas,

Cézanne, Matisse, Dalí, and Pollock. Recreations? Forgeries? Surely not originals! Track lighting in the ceiling created a calming ambience with accent lighting giving each seeming masterwork its own special glow.

'This is a place of reflection,' Mother said. 'Of retreat.'

'These *can't* be real,' I said, shaking my head, which was spinning with impossible, beautiful images.

'Oh but they can be, dear, and I would venture to say they are.'

I threw a hand toward an apparent Picasso. 'How in heaven's name could Colette *afford* all of this? Who on this *planet* could afford all of this?'

'No one,' Mother admitted. 'Such works are rarely for sale and, when they are, the auction prices they command are astronomical.'

I turned to her with my arms spread and my hands open. 'Then what explains it?'

I followed along as Mother strolled; we might have been in a fine museum on a Sunday afternoon, pausing at this painting or that, a Van Gogh flower bed depicted in screaming colors, Degas ballerinas on stage, a blue Matisse nude.

Then she stopped suddenly and her eyes locked with mine.

'My guess, dear? These are the spoils of many decades of fencing in the art business, going back decades, well before Colette Dumont was born.' She gestured grandly. 'If these paintings were to be researched, they would be on Interpol lists of stolen works, or in some cases – perhaps *many* cases – would expose paintings hanging in some of the most renowned museums as fakes.'

'Very good, Mrs Borne,' Colette said, behind us.

We both jumped, then turned. She was a few feet inside the door we'd entered through, accompanied by a small automatic pistol. She looked as lovely and composed as ever, but something about her eyes was . . . different.

The coldness seemed to dance with flames of fire in the irises.

'You know, Vivian,' she said conversationally, moving deeper into her private chamber, but slowly, 'you didn't need to go to so much trouble. You could have come in the front door – I mean, I left it unlocked for you, with the security system off. Surely you knew, even with this room tucked away as it is . . . that I'd *have* to have state-of-the-art security.'

'Of course,' Mother said, glancing about. 'Just as this room is climate-controlled, with attention to temperature and humidity – the key measures of environmental control.'

Mother was stalling, of course. Her hands were behind her back – and I had to give it to her: she had her cell out! Had she taken it from her pocket back in the library, the moment she realized we might have walked into a trap?

She was saying, 'I would imagine, Colette, that there are a thousand things you have to keep in mind, maintaining a secret, private collection like this. It must require an incredible attention to detail.'

'I should have paid better attention to one other detail at least,' Colette admitted. 'I expected your visit, I paved the way for it . . . but I *am* surprised you found your way into my, well, private little world – I *must* do something about that code in the future. What kind of fool would use their own phone number for security purposes?'

Mother and I would talk about that later. If there was a later.

'Oh, and Vivian? If that's your phone you're fiddling with behind your back? Don't bother. These walls are much too thick.'

While the cat had left us and defected to its master, Sushi had positioned herself mid-room between us and Colette, a few feet in from where our captor had entered, the door yawning open behind her onto the Jaguar-less chamber. No stranger to the sight of a gun, the little dog sent her eyes from me to Colette and back again, her ears perked.

Mother said, looking from wall to astonishing wall, 'You do know that all of this is in danger of coming down around you – nothing is more disruptive to careful planning than an impromptu murder or two. Dear, might I make a suggestion?'

Colette said nothing; her face seemed to be hardening further, if that were possible.

'You could really use a partner along about now,' Mother said. Her hands were out from behind her back now, her phone in one hand, casually at her side. '*Two* partners, actually, although my daughter is strictly support staff. With our shop, we could provide a new conduit for you, since – after suspicion inevitably descends upon you, even if you wriggle your way out – your Iowa City gallery will no longer be a viable front.'

A thin smile etched itself on the hard face. 'No good, Vivian. Nicely performed, if a little desperate . . . but no.'

Now and then Mother could underplay a scene admirably; this was one of those times.

'But I'm quite serious, Colette,' she said. 'I have the greatest admiration for you, which has only grown with what I've learned today. We're perfectly positioned to help you continue with your business. We'd be the ideal buffer – you'd be strictly a silent partner.'

Colette's shake of the head was punctuated by a softly musical laugh. 'Vivian, even if I believed any of this, I'm at a time of my life where, if I can weather this little storm, I can retire and enjoy the spoils of my labors. I won't be your silent partner, I'm afraid. But you and your daughter will be mine.'

The nose of the automatic rose.

Mother asked, 'How will you explain our . . . silence?'

'You'll be shot as burglars,' Colette said, as matter-of-fact as if she were explaining the specifics of this chamber's controlled climate. 'But, naturally, you'd can't be found in here.' She gestured with the weapon toward the open door behind her. 'Ladies . . . *move.*'

We did so.

But I took the lead. As I neared Colette, she moved sideways a bit, for me to go on through that door into the garage. She had the gun angled my way, apparently perceiving me as a greater threat than Mother – probably a mistake. There were two greater threats to her in her private chamber, and the biggest one was a little furry four-legged animal named Sushi.

I gave a sharp whistle, and Sushi darted for Colette, sinking razor-sharp teeth into the soft flesh of an ankle, making the woman howl, the gun suddenly, reflexively lowering. I stepped to one side and the second threat, Mother – with a pitch that could have landed her a spot on any Triple A baseball team

– flung that cell phone at Colette and hit her square in the forehead with it, stunning her.

Grabbing the nearest painting from its hook on the wall, I clobbered our staggered hostess with it, the canvas splitting, her head popping out and becoming the face of that blue Matisse nude before the torn canvas made its way down below and around her shoulders, trapping her upper torso within the frame. The impact sat her on the floor, hard, legs akimbo, very undignified for such an outwardly classy lady.

Mother snatched the automatic from the woman's limp fingers, and said to me, 'A little rash with that painting, dear. But I'm sure a good restorer can fix it in a jiffy.'

'Maybe you need a better support staff.'

'No, I'm quite satisfied with the one I have.'

We smiled at each other.

With the weapon now trained on the groggy Colette, Mother's question was nonetheless for me. 'May I, dear?'

'My pleasure.'

'Colette Dumont,' Mother said with a grin that was demented even for her, 'you're nicked!'

A Trash 'n' Treasures Tip

Over his lifetime Frank Lloyd Wright built 270 homes, many coming on the market for sale in recent years. Both Mother and I had always dreamed of living inside one of his fabulous creations, but could never afford to. Last Christmas I did my best and bought her the LEGO kit for Fallingwater House. Guess how I spent Christmas morning? That's right – building it for her!

TWELVE
Carry On at Your Convenience

Vivian Borne speaking, or I should say writing. I must thank my daughter for passing her mother (*moi*) the narrative ball, something she rarely does when we have both witnessed the same event. After all, the contracts for these books began with her, and continue to bear only her signature. So much as it does sometimes frustrate me, certain decisions about what goes into these books are hers, as the partner legally responsible for their content.

Her only proviso this time is that I make clear that certain aspects of my account – reporting actions of mine in the aftermath of this affair – were my own alone, undertaken without her knowledge. She asked me, in no uncertain (if rather emotional) terms not to include . . . well, I'm getting ahead of myself.

The morning after we handed Colette Dumont over to representatives of the Johnson County sheriff's department, Brandy and I were seated in Chief Tony Cassato's office, having been summoned there by him.

MI5 Agent Hasty was on speaker phone.

'Ladies,' the agent said, in that delightfully crisp British accent of his, 'although I can hardly condone your methods, I do want to thank you for helping expose, and putting an end to, the so-called American Connection in a notorious stolen art ring we have been after for decades.'

'Any time,' I said.

Brandy said nothing. Her demeanor was reminiscent of a schoolgirl summoned to the Principal's office.

Hasty continued: 'This criminal enterprise began in Paris with François Dumont, Colette's father, and has spanned more than five decades.' The agent paused. 'MI5 is sincerely grateful to you and your daughter, as are the various museums and private collectors who will at last have their precious art returned.'

When Hasty didn't continue, I asked, 'And that's all we get?'

'Ma'am?'

'That's all? Your sincere thanks? What about a reward? We are talking here about the recovery of millions in stolen goods.'

'Your "reward,"' Hasty said, 'which has been tentatively agreed upon by the various agencies involved – from Interpol to the sheriff's department in Iowa City – is that you will face no criminal charges for breaking and entering.'

'There was entering but no breaking,' I said, and I'm afraid it came out a trifle huffy. 'And, anyway, Colette left the door open for us. We were expected.'

'But you entered through a *coal* shoot, I understand.'

'More an aperture.'

The next came clipped: 'Were you expecting perhaps a medal?'

'Recognition *would* be nice,' I admitted. 'Possibly a People's Honour, or Royal Victorian Order . . .'

Tony was shaking his head at me, glaring.

'. . . but that, uh, will not be necessary. I will settle for learning why military security got involved in a criminal investigation in the first place. Shouldn't that have been New Scotland Yard's province?'

Silence from the speaker phone. Tony wasn't glaring now – his narrow-eyed expression indicated, if anything, an interest mirroring my own.

Then, from all the way from across the pond, came: 'Very well, Mrs Borne. I will provide no details, but *can* give you this basic information – funds from the sale of certain stolen art appear to have been funneled into terrorist activities in the UK.'

'I suspected as much,' I said. 'Can you tell me how Humphrey Westcott's murder factored in? He seems an unlikely figure to be connected to terrorism.'

'As far as we know, at this juncture, Mrs Borne, he was not. He appears to have been a cog in the ring who got too greedy.'

If they had allowed Brandy and me to stay in the UK, we could have cleared that up, too.

Speaking of Brandy, she came out of her shell long enough to pose a question: 'Agent Hasty, was Colette Dumont aware of these terrorist activities?'

'We can't be sure at this stage.'

'What is your guess? Your educated guess?'

'Mrs Borne, it's of our opinion the Dumont woman was not cognizant of the terrorism aspect . . . which is also the opinion of our sister organization, as well.'

Some sister! MI6, known in some quarters as The Circus.

Hasty said, 'I believe this concludes the conversation on our end. And . . . Vivian, Brandy . . . should you ever return to London, please let me know so I can make arrangements . . .'

Theater tickets, perhaps? A complimentary meal at the fabled Rules? Or – dare I dream it – a tour of the MI5 facility!

'. . . to put every law enforcement department at our disposal on high alert.'

Brandy smiled, but I didn't think his remark at all funny.

'Also, ladies,' Hasty said, and something friendly and – dare I say? – appreciative came into his voice, 'consider yourselves as having an open invitation to return, all expenses paid. We've made arrangements with the Savoy, and it's within our budget to provide transportation with British Airways as well.'

I sat up. 'First Class?'

'. . . First Class. Is that acceptable, madam?'

'Tickety boo!' I said.

The connection ended.

Brandy said, smiling, 'I can't believe you got First Class tickets out of him.'

'We've recovered millions for the poor sods, dear. At least we can get a little leg room out of it.'

The chief had yet to berate us for our latest sleuthing endeavors; but, for the nonce at least, he seemed to be setting that aside.

Instead he said, 'You may be interested to know that I had a chance to interview Angela James.'

Brandy sat forward, no longer in Principal's office mode. 'I'm not sure I completely understand Angela's role in all of this.'

I asked the chief, 'Is she being cooperative?'

He nodded. 'I'd say she sees the advantage of possibly lowering her sentence.'

Confused (poor dear), Brandy asked, 'Sentence for what?'

Tony's eyebrows rose, just a little. 'Accessory to murder after the fact. She was aware her husband killed Ruth Hassler.'

'Oh,' Brandy said.

'And she also knew of Skylar's involvement in Colette's business of procuring stolen works of art and high-ticket collectibles – including rare books.'

'Is that where the *Orient Express* comes into it?'

I let Brandy ask that – I felt I already knew, but we could (as we say in the trade) get the straight skinny from the horse's mouth (excuse the mixed metaphor), as she was the filly to best do it.

Tony paused, then spilled: 'After Ruth Hassler refused to sell the Christie book to her, Colette brought Skylar into the ring by enlisting his help in stealing it.' A shrug. 'According to Angela, the Hassler woman was supposed to be asleep, but surprised him at the top of the stairs, and he impulsively pushed her down.'

I asked, 'Was Tiffany James involved in any of this?'

After all, something had to have been weighing heavily on her mind.

'Yes,' Tony said. 'She provided Skylar with a key to her mother's house. That would make her guilty of felony murder – a death caused during the commission of a felony.'

Brandy said, 'What was her husband Jared's role in all this?'

'Nothing criminal,' Tony said. 'He was in a way a victim, in the sense that his wife was having an affair with Michael Hughes, and planned to dump her husband for the older man. Apparently, Jared wasn't aware of the money Tiffany siphoned off from her inheritance, which she socked away in that money market account with her lover's name on it.' Tony huffed a humorless laugh. 'Jared was like everybody else in this thing, in a way – all of them were in over their heads.'

'Not Colette,' I said. 'She always kept *her* head well above water.'

Brandy said, 'Not lately she didn't.'

'You're right,' the chief told his intended. 'Colette crossed what was apparently a new line for herself when, after talking to Skylar, she realized Tiffany had become a liability.'

'Poisoning the young woman,' I said, 'at the preview sale.'

Tony confirmed this with a somber nod.

I asked, 'Has the poison been identified?'

'Not as yet. But common ones such as cyanide and arsenic have been ruled out.'

I avoided Brandy's eyes.

'As for Skylar,' Tony said, 'after failing to obtain the cover to the Christie book, he'd become a liability himself, apparently.'

Especially if Skylar had told Colette that *I'd* mentioned MI5's interest in his connection to Humphrey Westcott.

Tony was saying, 'Colette's made no admissions, at least not as yet . . . but all of this is what we theorize, based in part on Angela revealing Skylar had broken his agreement with Colette.'

Frowning, Brandy asked, 'In what way?'

'He was never to display conspicuously stolen art where someone else might see it. Skylar had acquired a valuable Remington original from Colette, which was hanging in his office, where any number of people might see it.'

'And that got him killed?'

Tony nodded gravely. 'On such a rarefied level of dealing in illegal art, his unreliability must have been a major factor.'

Brandy was shaking her head. 'That doesn't make sense to me . . .'

'May I?' I asked the chief.

He nodded his assent.

'Dear,' I said to my less than worldly daughter, 'there are wealthy people in the world who will purchase art *not* as an investment, nor for braggadocio, but solely for their own personal enjoyment – just as Colette enjoyed her private collection in her "bunker."'

'How can that work?' Brandy asked. 'What happens when

one of these weird rich collectors die? What do their families do with these . . . these tainted masterpieces?'

Tony said, 'The art may go back onto the black market . . . or to be quietly, discreetly returned to the rightful owners, on the promise of no embarrassing publicity.'

'Or,' I interjected, 'if the rich collector knows the end is nearing, whether due to old age or infirmity, he or she might sell the plunder back to Colette or someone like her, possibly in accordance with the original agreement.'

'Well,' Brandy said, rolling her eyes, 'it sounds like sheer lunacy to me.'

I arched a brow. 'To you it does. But to a certain breed of collector? Nothing could feel more sane. Imagine feasting your eyes every day on a masterpiece that would otherwise have been unattainable – to smile back enigmatically at the Mona Lisa, perhaps, or trade glances with Van Gogh's self-portrait. Such collectors care not a whit what happens to their precious collections after they're gone. You can't take it with you!'

Brandy sucked in air. 'Good heavens! What about that painting I hit Colette with? *Can* it be restored? Or was it ruined?'

Tony bestowed a benevolent smile upon his future bride. 'That Matisse nude should be fine, after restoration. I spoke personally with the curator of the museum in Boston where it was stolen in 1990, and he was thrilled with its recovery, along with four other paintings taken at the time.'

The door of the conference room opened and a tall male officer I knew as Munson* stuck his head in.

'Chief, sorry to interrupt,' he said, 'but you're needed.'

'But we no longer seem to be,' I said, and stood. So did Brandy.

I said pleasantly, 'Until next time, Chiefie dear?'

But the busy lawman said nothing, merely closed his eyes and pointed to the door.

That afternoon, I was seated at a table in an interview room in the Johnson County Jail in downtown Iowa City, waiting patiently for Colette, being held there for the murders of Tiffany Wallace and Skylar James.

Other than her temporary court-appointed attorney, I was the only person she'd agreed to talk to, which I suppose was an honor of sorts. Since Brandy had gone to bed with a migraine right after our visit with Chief Cassato and Agent Hasty, I (in my role as ex-officio sheriff) commandeered the Fusion to make the journey.

The steel door with Plexiglas window opened, and Colette – in the expected if not terribly stylish orange jumpsuit – was escorted in by a sturdy female security guard with short dark hair and an unexpectedly kind face.

'Five minutes, Mrs Borne,' the guard said. 'I'll be just outside.' She departed, the door locking loudly behind her.

Colette slid into the chair across from me.

Without her high heels, designer clothes, and skillful make-up, the owner of Antiques Fantastique looked much older and smaller, her expression a defeated, melancholy thing. One could hardly blame her. Well, for the murders one could.

'I feel I owe you an apology, Mrs Borne,' Colette said, speaking softly. 'You were an able adversary, whereas I mistook you for a . . .'

She searched for the word, so I provided one: 'Buffoon?'

That actually made her smile. She said, 'I hope I would not be so unkind. Let us say, "rank amateur."'

'*I* would say, with all due respect, that you are the amateur in this situation . . . in murder, that is. Not in criminal enter-prise, of course, where you are a longtime expert. But you stepped out of your comfort zone when you dabbled in homicide.'

She was studying me. 'Are you wired, Vivian?'

'No. I'm always a little excited like this.'

'What I mean to say is, have you accessorized that, uh, lovely pants suit with a hidden microphone?'

'Heavens no! I can't be expected to do *all* of the work for the police. Ah . . . I understand. You and your attorney haven't settled on a plea as yet.'

'I haven't settled on an attorney as yet.'

I sat forward a little. 'I can recommend a good one. He's getting a touch on in years, but he can get even the most blatant murderess off. I'll make the referral if you like.'

'I'll get back to you on that.'

I shrugged. 'Anyway, if I were wired in the manner you suggest, your question and my denial would make this entrapment, and anything you say couldn't and wouldn't be used against you in a court of law. So you may speak freely with me, Colette. May I continue you to call you "Colette?"'

'Certainly.' She sighed. 'You are turning out to play a significant role in my life, actress that you are. The ease with which you accomplished my downfall makes me suspect some part of me wanted to be caught. I've grown so very, very *tired* of my whole way of life.'

Nodding understandingly, I let her talk.

She was looking past me, into memory. 'Back when my father ran the organization, people honored their agreements, as a matter of pride. But nowadays, no one can be trusted – everyone has their own agenda.'

I asked, 'Were you aware that art was being sold to raise money for terrorist acts?'

'Of course not!'

'Why the Christie book? Such an insignificant item, compared to a Matisse or Picasso.'

She shrugged. 'Not every sale in my field takes place on a stratospheric level. But signed copies in dust jacket of certain titles are nothing to sneeze at.'

That cheap reprint on British Air that crumbled in my hands was!

She was saying, 'I had a standing order for a signed *Orient Express* from a trusted client when Skylar told me he knew where to get one. That became his first assignment.' Her voice turned bitter. 'Which he bungled by killing that old woman.' She went on, 'Then, when an opportunity presented itself to get a cover for the book – provided by Humphrey Westcott – I gave Skylar a second chance after he mentioned that you were heading over to London. Why put my trust in the mail?' She sucked in air, let it out. 'Well, Skylar bungled that, too. And, after Tiffany's . . . death, he wanted out of our arrangement.'

So she was still reluctant to describe Tiffany's passing as the murder it was.

I asked, 'Is Michael Hughes involved in your business?'

'Who?'

'The auction house man who ran the tag sale.'

'Oh, *him* . . .' She shook her head. 'I barely know the man. He's nobody.'

Maybe, but a nobody who'd just come into a quarter of a million dollars. Chump change in her world, maybe, but then soon she'd be saving up dimes and quarters to buy candy bars from the prison canteen.

Colette straightened in her chair. 'Vivian, I feel I've said enough. Any debt I might have to you, for what I put you and your daughter through yesterday, you will have to consider settled. I'm tired and want to go back to my cell.'

'Your cell.' I smiled sadly. 'That's what you have to look forward to for the remainder of your days, isn't it? Of course, you've lived a fairly isolated life for years, and seem to have preferred the solitude of your own company, surrounded by beautiful works of art. So perhaps you're well prepared for what's ahead. Perhaps you'll get a talented graffiti artist for a cellmate . . . or maybe you can find some other way to dress up the dreary surroundings. Toward that end, I've brought you something.'

She said, skeptically, 'Kind of you, Vivian.'

I reached beneath the table, and placed the gift before her: a clear-plastic-wrapped bouquet of blue flowers I'd picked from her garden an hour earlier.

I said, 'I thought these might help.'

After several long moments that seemed to hang there in time, she smiled knowingly. 'They might. They might.'

I continued to hold onto them. 'Sorry there's no vase. That's not allowed. But you *are* able to have these. I've cleared it with the guard.'

I'd promised *her* the role of Grushenka, hoping that wouldn't catch up with me, like Colette's life of crime had caught up with her!

I said, 'I thought they were an option you might like to have – for freshening up your cell.'

The violet eyes locked with my blue ones. 'Thank you, Vivian. That really is a thoughtful gesture.'

'It's the least I could do . . . though perhaps in gratitude, you might be willing to share with me information regarding where some of the works you've distributed to private collectors might be found. By others who are into art?'

Colette didn't miss a beat. 'You'll find a ledger in a panel behind the books on the first shelf on the west wall in the library.'

I pushed the bouquet toward her. 'Thank you, dear.'

She was talking to herself now, shaking her head. 'It was so simple. It should have worked.'

I stood. 'You made one mistake, dear.'

She looked up. 'What's that?'

'You involved Vivian Borne.'

The door opened, the guard announcing my time was up.

As was Colette's.

Brandy back.

Don't you hate it when a story has obviously reached its natural conclusion, and yet still drags on and on? At least Archie Goodwin (actually Rex Stout) would label 'The Last Chapter' accordingly, so readers wouldn't get too antsy. Plus, Rex and Archie always keep the wrap-up short.

Having been down with a well-earned migraine for the entire afternoon, I awoke headache-free to find a text waiting from Tony.

My initial pleasant reaction curdled – it's never a good sign in a relationship when one's significant other says (or texts), 'We need to talk.' Tony's ominous words at least included a reminder of the dinner at his cabin that we'd planned (what now seemed like) eons ago.

Mother and I had ensnared a murderer in the trap that murderer had laid for us; but I was the one who seemed to be facing a last meal before her execution.

Downstairs I found Mother in a particularly good mood, and informed her of my upcoming evening with Tony. She said she'd heat up some leftovers for herself.

I returned upstairs, showered, fixed my hair, applied make-up, and put on something nice – not hoping to prevent the break-up exactly, rather trying to buy myself a little dignity when I faced the firing squad.

Taking Sushi along to keep Rocky busy, I went out to the Fusion, where I noticed three things: the driver's seat had been moved back, the gas gauge read near empty, and a pair of gardening gloves and shears were in the back.

OK, so Mother had needed to go somewhere, always a possibility when I was indisposed. But she'd made it back with herself and the car in one piece, so I would put her misconduct aside for now. Anyway, if the local cops and the Highway Patrol hadn't expressed an objection, why should I?

Taking the River Road again, I wondered if this scenic drive I so loved would forever be linked in my mind with Skylar's death. But the magnificent purple-pink rays of the sunset reflecting on the Mississippi, along with the casting of long shadows deepening the colors of the trees, erased such a notion. The turn was up ahead.

Life goes on.

I rumbled along the dirt lane leading to Tony's remote hide-away, then pulled up in front of the cabin, fully prepared that my role in Mother's dangerous detective work would lead to me getting dressed down by Tony (and not in the good way), capped by the cancelation of our engagement.

Sushi, well attuned to my moods, had been subdued on the familiar trip; but any concern for her mistress evaporated the moment we entered the cabin and she saw Rocky.

The black-and-white mixed breed with a K.O. circle around one eye had learned the best way to deal with Sushi's amorous pawing was to lie down and play dead until the poor thing had exhausted herself. Maybe I should try that approach.

Meanwhile, I just stood there, taking the room in.

I was going to miss the pleasant, woodsy smell of the place and its man's man ambience – Tony's collections of old fishing lures, wicker creels, and nets haphazardly nailed to the walls; the over-stuffed brown couch where he and I had spent many an hour in front of a crackling fireplace; the scarred round oak table and chairs where we shared dinners; the tiny kitchen where we often cooked together . . . out of which right now wafted the delicious aroma of his signature lasagna.

Serenity's Chief of Police appeared in the kitchen doorway, wearing the frilly apron I'd once given him as a joke, which made me smile even in these circumstances.

'Help me with the salad?' he asked.

One last time?

Always difficult to read, Tony seemed unexpectedly relaxed, upbeat. Perhaps he was relieved to be done with the needy likes of me . . . and Mother.

'Sure,' I said.

Everything was set out on a cutting board, and – as I started to chop the vegetables – he asked, 'Everything all right?'

I put the knife down. 'You tell me.'

Tony frowned. 'Oh.'

'Yes, oh. "We have to talk," you said. Texted, no less. Anyway, I'd prefer not to suffer through dinner.'

He put his bear-claw hands on my shoulders and looked down into my face, the steel-gray eyes boring through me. I felt suddenly very small.

'Am I am upset that you put your life in danger?' he asked. 'And that you and Vivian broke the law in your methods?'

'Are those rhetorical questions?'

'No. But don't answer them. I will. Yes. And yes.'

I feared as much.

Then he said, 'But I *had* asked for Vivian's help. And even though she promised to keep you out of harm's way, I would have to be crazier than she is to expect that she'd honor that. So that's on me.'

Was that the governor of the state on the line? Was this a reprieve?

His eyes softened. 'You did warn me, remember? When we first started dating? That your mother would come first. I understood that – not that it made things any easier.'

It *was* a reprieve!

'All I ask,' he went on, 'is that you try harder to keep her out of trouble, and yourself from getting caught up in her, her . . .'

'Shenanigans?'

'"Shenanigans" don't generally include having a little dog save your pretty bottom from a murderer about to shoot you.'

'Actually, more than once it has.' I put my arms around his waist. 'I'll do better.'

After the delicious meal, and when the dishes were done, Tony and I withdrew to the couch. Sushi was already snuggled against Rocky on the rug in front of the hearth, a crackling fire banishing the evening's chill.

We were discussing possible wedding dates when his cell vibrated.

Tony looked at the screen.

'Johnson County Sheriff,' he said to me. 'I've got to take this.'

Tony got up, and moved a discreet distance away, so I could only hear his end of the conversation.

'Yes . . .*What?*'

Something was up.

'Colette Dumont was found dead in her cell?'

Uh-oh.

'Vivian Borne came to see her?'

The near empty gas in the car.

'And brought what kind of flowers?'

The garden gloves and shears in the back seat.

I could draw only one conclusion.

I stood, scooped up Sushi, grabbed my purse, and headed toward the front door, Tony calling out behind me.

'*Brandy!*'

Stay tuned . . .

(Postscript: If you're thinking that Mother and I stood to collect hundreds of thousands of dollars, even millions, in reward money, for information leading to the recovery of so many stolen paintings . . . think again. Because of her irrevocable Honorary Sheriff status, Mother (and her deputy, me) were ineligible for such rewards. Bummer.)

A Trash 'n' Treasures Tip

Collecting old fishing lures can be a fun hobby, and also profitable. Many antique lures are worth hundreds, if not thousands, of dollars. The rarest of them all, a copper Giant Haskell Minnow, sold at an auction for over one-hundred-hundred thousand. That's a lot of bread on the hook. But think of all the reward money that slipped off ours!

BARBARA ALLAN is a joint pseudonym of husband-and-wife mystery writers, Barbara and Max Allan Collins.

BARBARA COLLINS made her entrance into the mystery field as a highly respected short story writer with appearances in over a dozen top anthologies, including *Murder Most Delicious, Women on the Edge, Deadly Housewives* and the bestselling *Cat Crimes* series. She was the co-editor of (and a contributor to) the bestselling anthology *Lethal Ladies,* and her stories were selected for inclusion in the first three volumes of *The Year's 25 Finest Crime and Mystery Stories.*

Two acclaimed collections of her work have been published – *Too Many Tomcats* and (with her husband) *Murder – His and Hers*. The Collins's first novel together, the Baby Boomer thriller *Regeneration,* was a paperback bestseller; their second collaborative novel, *Bombshell* – in which Marilyn Monroe saves the world from World War III – was published in hardcover to excellent reviews. Both are back in print.

Barbara also has been the production manager and/or line producer on several independent film projects.

MAX ALLAN COLLINS was named a Grand Master by the Mystery Writers of America in 2017. He has earned an unprecedented twenty-three Private Eye Writers of America 'Shamus' nominations, many for his Nathan Heller historical thrillers, winning for *True Detective* (1983), *Stolen Away* (1991), and the short story, 'So Long, Chief.'

His classic graphic novel *Road to Perdition* is the basis of the Academy Award-winning film. Max's other comics credits include 'Dick Tracy'; 'Batman'; his own 'Ms Tree'; and 'Wild Dog,' featured on the *Arrow* TV series.

Max's body of work includes film criticism, short fiction, songwriting, trading-card sets, and movie/TV tie-in novels, such as the *New York Times*-bestseller *Saving Private Ryan,* numerous *USA Today*-bestselling CSI novels, and the Scribe Award-winning *American Gangster*. His non-fiction includes *Scarface and the Untouchable: Al Capone* and *Eliot Ness & the Mad Butcher* (both with A. Brad Schwartz).

An award-winning filmmaker, he wrote and directed the Lifetime movie *Mommy* (1996) and three other features; his produced screenplays include the 1995 HBO World Premiere *The Expert* and *The Last Lullaby* (2008). His 1998 documentary *Mike Hammer's Mickey Spillane* appears on the Criterion Collection release of the acclaimed film *noir*, *Kiss Me Deadly*. The Cinemax TV series *Quarry* is based on his innovative book series.

Max's recent novels include a dozen-plus works begun by his mentor, the late mystery-writing legend, Mickey Spillane, among them *Masquerade for Murder* with Mike Hammer and the Caleb York western novels.

'BARBARA ALLAN' live(s) in Muscatine, Iowa, their Serenity-esque hometown. Son Nathan works as a translator of Japanese to English, with credits ranging from video games to novels.